The door between the bedroom and the small living room of the suite opened. Sadiq's heart sank. Framed in the doorway, like something out of a nightmare, stood a man in a balaclava helmet and a black wet suit. But this man was not dressed for swimming. Nor, for that matter, were the instruments in his hands designed for fishing.

Sadiq Ali Qadar knew, with a sudden cold conviction, that he was about to die.

For Alan Duncan

HAWL

JAMES PEACOCK

A STAR BOOK
published by
the Paperback Division of
W.H. Allen & Co. PLC

A Star Book
Published in 1986
by the Paperback Division of
W.H. Allen & Co. PLC
44 Hill Street, London W1X 8LB

Typeset in Plantin by Fleet Graphics, Enfield, Middlesex

Printed and bound in Great Britain by
Anchor Brendon Ltd, Tiptree, Essex

ISBN 0 352 1760 4

Chapter One

As Bert Thompson started to change down through the gears of his huge tanker in preparation to swinging round an approaching turn-off he had a momentary feeling that all was not well. Bert was in a bit of a hurry. His home was only a few miles from the turn-off and he did not have far to go now to make his delivery. He'd pop in and have a couple of hours with the wife before completing the run. As he swung the roaring giant into the turn it hit him – a smashing hammer blow in the chest which crushed the breath from him. Strange, tingling pains coursed his shoulders and arms. The strength fled from them. His hands fell from the wheel. As the agonising pressure on his chest increased his eyes blurred, his legs stiffened convulsively and his foot jammed down on the accelerator. He was dead as the tanker snarled round the bend and hurtled against a red telephone kiosk.

Inside the telephone box a dark haired young woman in a smart, boxy camel hair car coat was engaged in the process of dialling a London number. Some premonition of danger stilled her busy finger. The receiver held to her ear, she turned her head. She saw the huge truck mount the pavement and surge towards her. Frantically she dropped the instrument and tried to push her way out of the kiosk. In her panic she pushed desperately at the wrong panel. In the seconds it took to realise her mistake the tanker smashed into the telephone box ripping it from its anchors and carrying it forward for a moment before it began to disintegrate. The woman died instantly in the impact but, like some ravening beast, the tanker rolled over the wreckage and ground her to a pulp beneath its huge wheels before coming to a crunching rest halfway into the living room of a small cottage.

Death comes to us in a myriad ways. With some it is sudden, swift, unexpected oblivion arriving like a thunderbolt from nowhere, removing its victim with abrupt immediacy to leave stunned, bewildered dependants to cope as best they can with shattered lives. With others it follows in the wake of long, agonising illnesses with the spectre looming continuously for months. In such instances it is frequently received as a blessed relief, but mostly it is fought to the bitter, agonising end with grim, stubborn tenacity. There are some who depart this life with calm, deliberate dignity yielding gracefully to the inevitable. But they are not many. Jennifer Wilkinson, aged four, and her mother, Caroline, aged twenty-six, were not among this minority.

The bomb, a 1982 Ford Granada, its boot carefully packed with two hundred and twenty pounds of gelignite, was neatly and legally parked in a side street outside the West entrance to one of the city's largest stores. The clock on the dashboard, now telling a time of 11.49, was not the clock which had originally been purchased with the car. This clock, indistinguishable from the one it had replaced, had been very cleverly tampered with. A single extra lead of fine grey plastic sheathed wire snaked down from behind the dashboard to merge anonymously with a multitude of other similar wires. This extra wire, apparently no different from the many others it had joined, led directly to the electrically activated detonator buried in the heart of the gelignite. The Granada, which had originally been a faintly repulsive shade of red, was now a nondescript blue and carried license plates which were also strange to the vehicle. It had been stolen in Epsom some three weeks before and its owner, the wife of a city stockbroker, had given up all hope of ever seeing it again. She was currently engaged in the tedious, slightly distasteful business of nagging her husband into procuring a replacement.

But Caroline and Jennifer Wilkinson had no such problems. They were happily engaged in the process of wandering back down through the huge store aiming, eventually, for the West entrance and their neat little one-year-old Datsun Sunny parked a few yards away from the blue Granada. They had just spent a pleasant, if tiring hour searching for, and eventually finding, a suitable, not too expensive birthday gift for Jennifer's daddy who was due home in a few days following a four month stint in Nigeria.

Caroline Wilkinson, a trim, compact brunette, was, like her daughter (a miniaturised version of herself), very much looking forward to her husband's homecoming. Still very much in love with her burly five-foot ten-inch spouse after six and a half years of marriage, Caroline found herself wondering if they had done the right thing in leaving the service. At least for the best part of the time they had been together and they had liked Hereford. But the swift violence of the Falklands had been a little too much for her to take. Ireland was bad enough but the Falklands had been something else. To please her, Bill had resigned his commission and returned, hopefully to the profession he had originally espoused – engineering. But work, in a world fighting ferociously for economic stability, was far from plentiful, which was why her husband, fourteen years her senior, had wound up a Project Engineer with an Oil Company.

Three times a year, under the terms of his contract, the little family had a few weeks together. Four months did not seem a long time for them to be separated but, in reality, it seemed to stretch endlessly ahead like a dark, lonely century. This time though, things would be different. Bill, while still employed by the Nigerian company, had been given what amounted to a home posting. He had been given a new project which had to be designed in the London Office. This meant he would be home for at least eighteen months. Possibly longer because chances of promotion were much greater in London than sweating in the Niger Delta. Perhaps he would have to go back eventually but at least they would have eighteen months together and that, compared to the two or three weeks they normally had, seemed almost like a lifetime. Time enough to see Jennifer settled properly in school. Time, and she felt a delicious warm feeling at the thought, to set about producing a brother or sister for her daughter.

Caroline, her daughter's small hand held firmly in her own, paused a few moments to admire some particularly alluring lingerie. She was tempted - *very* tempted. She could just imagine Bill's reaction to her wearing some of the items on display. It would be swift and immediate. A smile tugged at the corners of her soft mouth. Perhaps his reaction would be too swift and too immediate. With something approaching a giggle she turned away from the slightly erotic display and led her wide-eyed daughter through the milling bargain hunters towards the West entrance.

Inside the Granada the clock on the dashboard showed thirty seconds to noon.

At twelve minus ten seconds Caroline and Jennifer, smiling at an elderly gentleman who politely held the door open for them, stepped hand in hand into the side street. They would get out of the busy city centre, have a quiet lunch somewhere, then take it easy back to Croydon. They paused momentarily on the kerb to check the approaching traffic in the one-way street.

Both hands on the Granada clock became absolutely vertical. Inside the clock two tiny strips of copper suddenly made contact for the first time. All power from the twelve volt battery to the clock stopped, hesitated for a nanosecond then flashed to the new contact and leaped along the strange wire.

Caroline's shocked mind fleetingly registered the distintegration of the blue Granada. She did not hear the barking roar of the explosion because in the same microsecond she was aware of a momentary jarring blow before she was picked up and hurled backwards through huge plate glass windows already disintegrating inwards from the enormous force of the blast. She was only vaguely conscious of another jarring blow to her back and a sense of the air being sucked savagely from her lungs. That part of her mind which was a mother reacted instantaneously. Unaware she had less than twenty heartbeats to live she was conscious that she still held her daughter's warm little hand. Instinctively, protectively, she pulled the child towards her. Jennifer came easily. Too easily. Caroline Wilkinson's last living memory was the obscene sight of her daughter's severed arm held tightly in her own hand.

Mercifully, what Caroline never knew was that, in the same instant she was aware of the car exploding, a razor sharp, terribly distorted section of the rear wing was driven directly towards her. The metal, impelled with enormous force, cut Caroline in half, severed Jennifer's arm and, as a final act, completely decapitated the little girl. Jennifer's head, still smiling happily, clear hazel eyes wide open, was not, like the rest of her, hurled back into the charnel house of the store. Through some freak action the little head was lifted fully twenty-five feet in the air to fall, turning and spinning back into the gutter. It was later discovered by a grey-faced retching policeman resting against someone's discarded fish and chips.

Thirty-two people died in the blast. One hundred and fifteen were injured, thirty-nine of them severely. Five of these later succumbed to their injuries and seventeen were maimed for life including a sixteen-year-old salesgirl who lost both her hands and was blinded. There were no policemen and no servicemen among the dead or injured. The nearest the bomb had come to killing a member of the establishment had been the retired civil servant who had politely held open a door for a lovely young mother and her pretty, smiling daughter.

Britain and the rest of the Western World were stunned.

Following so closely upon a succession of bombings the sheer, mindless savagery of it left people with a sick, cold feeling in the pit of their stomachs. Where was it going to end? Where could it end? What could really be done in a world where any crazed psychopath could kill and maim under cover of some weird political goal which the people he killed had never even heard of? What could be done in a society where retribution was frequently neither swift nor just. Where terrorists, many of them multi-murderers, were simply locked up and cossetted for a few years? Where known terrorist leaders were allowed to walk the streets freely, become respected politicians, in some cases become leaders of their countries and actually be given aid by the very people they had encouraged their killers to murder at every opportunity?

For four days, while the world guessed, implied, and theorised, no political movement, outlawed or otherwise, claimed responsibility for what had come to be known as the

Granada Bomb. Then, on the morning of the fifth day, a spokesman for Sinn Féin the so-called political arm of the IRA, calmly announced the bombing had been carried out by soldiers of the provisional IRA. It had been a planned and authorised attack, he said, but something had gone wrong. The plan had called for a half-hour warning. For some reason, which was still being investigated, the warning had not been received. Meanwhile, he gave his most sincere apologies and condolences to those civilians who had been hurt or had lost a loved one in the struggle for a United Ireland.

Apologies!

As with the other bomb attacks a second wave of revulsion swept through the United Kingdom. There was much talk of outlawing Sinn Féin, even more talk of bringing back the death penalty. But, in the end, after much Westminster huffing and puffing and long-winded speeches about the reprehensible actions of utterly callous men, nothing was done.

Some six weeks following the Granada Bomb incident there began a series of apparently unrelated robberies which baffled the police of several counties in England and Scotland. Most were payroll hold-ups carried out by a single, balaclava-masked gunman armed with an ugly Kalashnikov. Three were Post Office robberies again carried out with considerable audacity by a single gunman and one was a bank hold-up carried out at a branch office of Barclays serving a large industrial estate. It was some three weeks before it crystallised in various police headquarters that they were dealing with what amounted to a one man country-wide crime wave. However, the fact that the gunman seemed to strike indiscriminately, often with as much as four hundred miles between crimes, made it exceedingly difficult for them to formulate any kind of coherent plan which might ultimately result in his capture. They were further handicapped by the fact that each crime had to be investigated locally and the incredible slowness involved in correlating reports centrally. Time was also very much against them in that two months after they had begun the robberies ceased.

In none of the twenty-eight incidents was a single person hurt seriously – although one payroll guard nursed an egg-sized lump on his head for a few days. The gross take for the robberies amounted to a very healthy £205,000, most of it virtually untraceable.

While British police forces heaved a sight of relief and got down to the desperately slow work of sifting through piles of reports and interviewing literally hundreds of witnesses, Interpol became alerted by a similar wave of incidents throughout Europe. Again the *modus operandi* was the same. A single masked gunman carrying a Kalashnikov. Once more the spate of robberies ceased after a few weeks.

Later, when it was finally admitted that the robberies on both sides of the Channel had quite possibly been committed by the same audacious character, it was calculated that his overall take amounted to over three-quarters of a million pounds, made up of various currencies, but all cash and all virtually untraceable. Investigations, of course, continued. But some four months after the spate of robberies began and roughly six months following the Granada bomb incident, the Kalashnikov robber ceased all activities. To all intents and purposes he vanished, presumably to live happily and comfortably on his ill-gotten gains.

Chapter Two

Roughly one hundred miles north along the A1, or what was once known as the Great North Road, there is a turn-off which leads eventually to a quiet little village called Roseford. If one takes a sharp left from what passes as Roseford's main street, one finds oneself on another narrow 'B' road leading to Upper Roseford some three and a half miles away. The cut-off for Upper Roseford is a sharp, right angled one and has to be negotiated reasonably carefully. Not so very long ago a fully loaded tanker ran out of control here, demolishing a telephone kiosk just beyond the corner and in the process killing young Miss McKinley from Ford Farm. Now, of course, there is no sign of the old telephone box and the new one, sited a hundred and fifty yards away, has been recessed into a five foot high cottage garden wall.

Roseford could never, by any stretch of imagination, be classified as anything other than sleepy. The modern equivalent of feudal peasants, the people who lived here were born of the land. Fiercely independent, they steadfastly minded their own business and expected strangers to reciprocate. Excitement in the village was invariably generated by Tommy Granger getting falling-down drunk in the Dun Cow of a Saturday, or the Widow Thompson from Upper Roseford (she who had been married to the driver of the tanker) being seen in the company of a man.

Generally speaking, very little disturbed the phlegmatic calm of the villagers. Even when something did they were very slow to react and the surface placidity seemed to bear scarcely a ripple. The death of young Miss McKinley had caused uneasy currents for a while but then it had been fairly generally agreed upon that it had partly been her own fault. She could quite easily have waited until she returned to the farm to make her call. That was the trouble with young people today. Always in a hurry, always had to get everything done straight away. Well, it had been the death of her in the end. If she'd settled for a few minutes' walk back to the farm she would have been alive today.

Bert Thompson now, well, he was another matter. Born and bred in Upper Roseford, Bert was. Who would ever have dreamed he had a bad heart? Always looked as strong as a horse, Bert did, and always a pleasant word for everybody. Still, he never should have married that flightly Mary Tirfor. Half his age she was. And wild too. She'd worn him out in the end – that's what had happened to Bert.

Apart from the violence of the accident little had stirred Roseford in the past for years save, of course, the arrival of the McKinleys themselves. And that had been nearly six years ago. They'd bought the old Ford farm. Not that it was a farm any more of course, only the old farmhouse sitting in about half an acre of assorted fruit trees about halfway between the two villages.

The McKinleys had come from one of the Scottish Islands originally. If you listened closely you could tell from the nice soft accent they had. Quite an arty-crafty bunch really. Not, heaven forbid, that they wore beads or had hair hanging down their backs. But Tom, the eldest brother, and Michael, the youngest, were both writers; Ian, the middle one, was some kind of antique specialist forever running about with all kinds of ancient looking rubbish in the back of his van; and young Morag, the one who was killed, hardly ever went anywhere without a sketch pad and you often used to see her out and about with her easel and paints.

Nice family though. Kept themselves to themselves and didn't try to pry into things which didn't concern them. Always had a smile for everybody and in spite of their arty-crafty background behaved just like ordinary folk. Didn't try to put on any airs and graces or imply they were in any way superior or different. Come down to the Dun Cow occasionally and mix in with the locals, they would. Young Michael was beginning to get a fearsome reputation at darts and none of them were slouches when it came to dominoes. Actually, if you didn't know better, you'd think they'd lived in Roseford all their lives.

But the steadfast calmness of Roseford was about to be disrupted. The sleepy little village which had remained much the same for over four hundred years would shortly be pitch-forked savagely into the twentieth century.

All that was left of Captain William Wilkinson tottered toward the green painted wrought iron gate of 47, Chestnut Avenue to pause a moment, wavering uncertainly on splayed, wobbling legs. Clinging desperately to a brown paper carrier bag obviously containing bottles he peered about him through unfocussed and distant eyes as if he were not quite certain he was in the right neighbourhood. Fair, formerly well-trimmed hair curling over his collar and dangling lankly across bloodshot, sunken eyes, traces of vomit on a blazer which looked as if he had slept in it, flies half-open and the tail of his shirt protruding, he was not a prepossessing sight. This was a far cry from the erect, immaculate Bill Wilkinson remembered by other residents of the Avenue. Slowly his free hand reached for the gate.

From the living room window of number 46 on the other side of the Avenue Anne Parkinson watched his wavering attempts to grasp the latch. Pursing her lips slightly, she drew her finely drawn eyebrows together in a slight frown. The unkempt figure missed the latch, lurched, and almost fell across the gate. Anne gasped and unconsciously her hand flew to her mouth. Her brother Gerald, curious as to what kept her stationed by the window, uncoiled his lean six foot from a comfortable armchair and crossed the room to stand beside her.

'Oh, Christ,' he said quietly. 'Not again.'

Some slight inflection in her brother's voice alerted the young woman. She turned her expensively coiffed auburn head and shot her brother a curious glance. 'What do you mean, not again, Gerry?'

The tall man glanced across at the wavering figure. For a moment a shadow darkened his eyes. 'A pretty grim story, really,' he said, a tentative, half grin at his mouth. 'But with you busy becoming so famous on the other side of the Atlantic you wouldn't know about it.'

Across the road Wilkinson managed to get the gate open. Anne momentarily felt like cheering. She wrinkled her pert nose at her brother causing him to grin once more, a little more wholeheartedly this time. Anne, a popular television reporter, and her brother, something in the Foreign Office, were as close as their respective careers permitted them to be. The nose-wrinkling was one of many teasing signals between them stretching back to the time when a nine-year-old boy discovered it was going to be virtually impossible to escape from a five-year-old sister.

'Come on, Gerry. What goes on with that man across the way?'

They watched Wilkinson stagger up the garden path toward the door of number 47. Gerald cleared his throat.

'Up until two months ago, Anne, yon alcohol-soused gentleman used to live in that house.'

'Used to?' Anne queried, watching the drunk begin to search his pockets, presumably for a key.

'Used to,' her brother repeated grimly. 'That man is William Wilkinson. He and his family lived in that house. Very proud of it they were too. The thing was, Wilkinson was an engineer, ex-army type, and he worked in Africa some place – Nigeria, I think. Now, that meant they didn't have a great deal of time together really because Wilkinson only got home every three or four months. But even at that they all seemed to be terribly fond of each other and Wilkinson yonder spent every moment of the time he was home with them.' He sighed. 'Anyway, to cut a long story short, his wife and little girl were killed in the Granada thing just four days before he came home. Rather a bloody mess from what I can gather.

'Wilkinson just went to pieces. Hit the bottle like it was going out of style. Well, finally, I suppose, he simply ran out of money. First the car, then the house were sold from under him and yonder you see the result. He's never one hundred percent sober and every so often he comes home – just like he's doing now. I don't think he really knows where he is any more. Or even who he is, for that matter.'

Anne Parkinson's green eyes softened compassionately as she saw some kind of lost, bewildered comprehension dawn on the drunk's unshaven face. His shoulders slumped even further and he staggered dazedly away from the once welcoming door. Yet, compassion aside, another part of her mind was busy telling her there was a story here. Here was the side of terrorism nobody ever really saw. What *really* happened to those widows, widowers, bereaved parents? What actually happened to their lives after the first few brave words for the media? Anne's compassion began to fade and was replaced by a calculating thoughtfulness. She watched the drunk shuffle back through the gate, sway uncertainly for a moment, then stagger off down the Avenue. The man's mouth appeared to be working as if he were mumbling to himself. Anne wished, momentarily, she were close enough to overhear his mouthings before she realised they were probably incoherent mumblings and not at all useful to her purpose.

Purpose? The young woman realised suddenly she had made her mind up. A hesitant, flickering thought had gained momentum and crystallised. There *was* a story. Perhaps even the basis for the book she kept promising herself she would write. She glanced again at her brother.

'You say that man – er – Wilkinson, keeps coming back here?'

'Sure,' Gerald nodded. 'His brain is so addled now he seems to return here by some kind of instinct. Like a bloody homing pigeon. This is the third time he's been back in just over a week. At least it's the third time I've seen him. He could have been here more often, of course. Pathetic really.'

Anne's calculating green eyes returned to the vanishing drunk. She nodded her head almost imperceptibly. There was no doubt in her mind: she and the staggering shambles of a man would meet. Soon!

Tim Carter of the *Express* fervently hoped he was not out in this weather on a wild goose chase. His undoubted ability to ferret out a good story gave him a considerable amount of leeway with his boss but he was expected to produce. Thanks to a couple of dead ends on the drug abuse thing he was working on he had not come up with very much in the past couple of weeks and was beginning to become slightly paranoid. The telephone call (passed to him by a busy operator) had not really given him much to go on. But, at the time, a gut feeling had nagged him into believing he was on to something big. Now he was not so sure the gut feeling had been anything more than hunger pangs.

The telephone message had been ludicrously brief. No introduction, no preliminaries. Just a simple statement made in an odd, flat monotone as if the speaker did not care whether he was listened to or not.

'If you are still interested in the people responsible for the Granada Bomb, go to Roseford and look for Ford Farm.'

That was it. Nothing else.

The caller, who sounded as if he might have caught a cold, immediately closed the connection before Tim had time to frame a question let alone ask it. Dependent a great deal upon tip-offs, either anonymous or otherwise, for his investigative work Carter had automatically switched on his recorder as he picked up the receiver. After listening to it again he took the tape to his editor, a dour, overworked Scot with a brain as sharp as his tongue. The Scot, his broad, blunt-fingered hands folded on the desk before him, heard the tape in silence.

'Well, what do ye think?' he barked suddenly.

Carter shrugged. 'Well, I think somebody should look into it.'

His editor nodded his big, grizzled head. 'Aye, so do I, laddie, so do I. I'll give ye two hours before I phone Special Branch. If ye do manage to get there before the police try and keep out o' trouble. Remember Sean McEwan is still on the loose.'

Halfheartedly Carter tried to back off. 'But I've got . . . '

'Ye've got nothing, laddie. Ye've been in the doldrums for days. Off with ye now.' He glanced at the watch on his thick, hairy wrist. 'Ye've got exactly two hours. I can't hold this any longer and I might be stretching my luck even at that.'

* * *

Roseford had not been hard to find in the big Road Atlas Carter kept in his desk. He had been a little disconcerted to discover several villages of the same name listed but, fortunately, only one within easy striking distance of the City. It had to be the one. Terrorists would want to be within easy striking distance of such a prime target.

Carter was only a little happier when he emerged from the pleasant warmth of the Dun Cow into a bitterly cold, black night of driving rain. The landlord, like most of his type, had been far from forthcoming. But at least he had admitted to there being a Ford Farm in the area and reluctantly parted with directions as to finding it.

In the event the farmhouse was not hard to find at all. Carter's headlights struck it immediately as he brought his Datsun 280 over a narrow, hump-backed bridge about two miles out of Roseford. An old, small windowed, two storey structure, it crouched a few yards from the edge of the road, facing into his lights. For some odd reason it reminded Carter of a large, wet, squatting toad.

The gateway, its four bar gate hanging crookedly open, bore a neatly painted but weatherworn sign: 'Ford Farm'. No lights glimmered in the windows. As Carter cruised past the gate he had the impression the place was deserted. On impulse he pulled off the road and stopped the car.

The rain continued to sheet heavily as Carter, still wondering if he was on a wild goose chase, alternately scrunched and squelched up the short drive to the house. For once the reporter was grateful at his wife's insistence that he carry a large flashlight in the car. Without it he would have failed to see his own hand held immediately in front of his face. The darkness was Stygian. The rain, lashing straight down upon a cringing world, was icy cold on the ungloved hand playing the torch beam on the roughly gravelled path before him.

Carter, despite his impression the place was deserted, found himself moving with an extra exaggerated caution as he approached and passed the grim, blank face of the gable end. He paused, listening, outside one of the heavily draped ground floor windows. Not a sound. Not a chink of light. Nothing save the incessant hiss of the rain and the heavier rush of water from a guttering drain pipe. A drop of icy water trickled under his raincoat collar and rolled coldly down the back of his neck. He shivered, and his reaction was not entirely due to the unexpected chill on his flesh.

Tim was suddenly uneasy. But, had he been asked why, he would have been unable to answer. He had an odd impression of wrongness. A chilling feeling that something was not quite right. He had to almost force himself away from the window. His feet were decidedly dragging as he followed the white beam of light from the torch.

The door was placed stolidly in the absolute centre of the face wall. It glittered with an ugly wet blackness as he played the torch over it. Carter might have stopped his legs from carrying him forward but almost as if they had a will of their own they bore him on. He saw, almost as if it belonged to someone else, his hand knock on the wet wood. The heavy door gave slightly under the blow. It was unlatched.

Unaware he was holding his breath the reporter pushed open the door wider. Aiming his torch through the gap he found himself looking directly into a small hall. A staircase, poorly carpeted, reached steeply upwards on the right. To the left a corridor stretched back to another door, probably the kitchen. Two ugly varnished doors led off to left and right directly from the hall. Carter stepped into the hall and immediately regretted doing so. There was something forbidding about the place. He could feel it. Ugly, menacing, pressing down on him like a blanket seeking to engulf and smother. He shivered again. It was almost as cold inside as out. He became aware of a familiar, cloying smell which he recognised but could not, for the moment, identify.

Urged on by something he was powerless to resist, Tim moved cautiously towards the door on his right. As he reached for the door handle and turned it the torch in his hand flickered and died. Probably the rain had got to it. Pushing open the door he stepped over the threshold. His foot brushed something to one side. Like a living thing the stench of urine, shit and something else rushed at him eager to escape the seal of the door. Gagging, he groped for the light switch.

Never, for as long as he lived, was Tim Carter to forget the horror of the room he stood in.

Now he recognised the cloying, coppery smell for what it was. Blood. The haunting smell of the butcher's shop. The room was literally drenched in it. Ceiling, walls, carpeted floor, even the partially wrecked furniture. He knew from a slight stickiness underfoot that he was standing in a pool of it. Remembering - probably subconsciously because his mind refused to accept what he was seeing - the object he had kicked as he entered the room, he glanced down.

The full horror of what he had discovered lanced like a tongue of flame into his brain. Just beside his right foot, crouching like a tiny animal, lay a severed hand palm down upon the carpet.

In the few palpitating seconds it took the reporter to absorb and recognise what he was seeing, it seemed to his frantic, reeling mind that the room was filled with bodies and parts of bodies. Limbs hurled carelessly about formed ugly, assymetrical patterns with broken or overturned furniture, and everywhere great dark patches of blood counterbalanced them. It was the centrepiece of the hideous tableau which dragged the horrified shriek from the very depths of his being.

From an upended table in the centre of the room, held securely in place by several six-inch nails, the naked body of a man faced him. Both the man's hands and feet were raw, ugly stumps where the fingers and toes had been removed. He had been crudely but efficiently castrated and his genitals lay alongside the stumps of his feet. The man's eyes were wide open and his face contorted into a terrible grimace of absolute horror. On his chest, carved neatly, and very carefully with a finely honed blade, were the letters *HAWL*.

Carter broke.

Vomiting and retching, the reporter fled stumbling and lurching into the blackness of the driving rain and the night. He was hardly aware of the three police cars turning into the drive or of the surprisingly gentle hands of two large, armed policemen as they led him to one of the vehicles.

Chapter Three

'MOST WANTED TERRORISTS MURDERED.'

So screamed the *Express* headlines the following morning. The story, probably one of the best the newspaper had a lead on for several weeks, continued:

'Last night following a lead given them by the *Express*, armed police raided a lonely farmhouse near Roseford in Rutland and discovered the mutilated bodies of Sean McEwan, James Reilly, and Thomas Flynn.

'McEwan, who had successfully evaded capture for seven years, was one of the most wanted men on police files. He is known to have been implicated in several bombings and was wanted for five murders.

'Reilly, sought for the bombings of a Belfast pub and the murder of two soldiers, had also been on the run for several years and was also known to have been implicated in several other bombings.

'Flynn, the youngest of the murdered men, was wanted for the murder of a policeman and the bombing of a department store which resulted in the deaths of two women.

'A fourth member of the group, now identified as Bridget Conolly, was accidentally killed several months ago when a tanker collided with a telephone box. Conolly was known to have lured at least one young soldier to his death.

'Large quantities of arms and explosives have been discovered in the farmhouse. A systematic search of the grounds is now under way.

'An interesting aspect of the crime is that Conolly was killed in a telephone box only half an hour prior to the infamous

Granada Bomb affair. Police now believe the gang was responsible for this act and Conolly was probably killed while attempting to make a warning telephone call.

'A police spokesman also admitted to the possibility of the gang having been killed by a rival organisation. This theory is to some extent borne out by the fact that the letters *HAWL* were left on the body of one of the dead men. There is, however, no record of any organisation known by this acronym. It is hoped this particularly brutal killing is not the long talked of Protestant backlash.'

The *Express*, hammering its undoubted scoop, then went on to describe the scene at the farmhouse with as much gory detail as it thought the British public could take with its breakfast. One paragraph described the newspaper's stance on the affair:

'It is doubtful if any right-minded citizen will mourn the passing of this group of killers. Now assumed to be responsible for the deaths of over fifty of our citizens while enjoying the hospitality of our shores, they will not be missed. Themselves meting out death and destruction by stealth and trickery, they came to their own ends in a similar manner. To many who have suffered as a result of their actions, justice, in a sense, will have been seen to have been done.'

Generally speaking, the long suffering British public, fed up to the teeth with the continuing mindless sectarian violence, was inclined to agree.

Sinn Féin was not.

The same spokesman, who had taken five days to crawl from under his stone over the Granada affair and who was a duly elected representative of his people, was on the telephone to the *Express* within an hour of receiving his copy of the newspaper. He spoke to the same grizzled veteran who had dispatched Tim Carter to Roseford. The Scot listened to the man rant on for several minutes. This time the wrathful Sinn Féin spokesman accused everyone from the Queen, through the SAS, to *Express* copy boys of complicity in the unholy murder of three brave soldiers of the IRA.

Finally when the duly elected Representative had finished, or perhaps simply run out of breath, the Scot said, with a fine sense of irony, 'Please convey the apologies of the *Express* to your people. We understand the matter is under investigation,' and hung up the receiver.

Special Branch, however, were not overjoyed. They were, in fact, very uneasy over the whole matter. Following several very top level discussions, a high ranking officer made his way to a very unprepossessing office off Horse Guards Parade. There, at approximately ten past four in the afternoon, he was ushered into the presence of Sir Thomas Griff with whom he remained tightly closetted until seven-thirty. At this time the meeting was moved to Sir Thomas's very exclusive club and continued over dinner. Around ten-thirty the Special Branch man left. Sir Thomas returned thoughtfully to his office where one of his three long suffering secretaries, just finishing her shift, made him a cup of coffee.

Sir Thomas sipped his coffee and smoked a Garcia and Vega Napoleon with a dedicated ferocity which filled the small office with a strangling fog. Presently he picked up the telephone and made two calls, one of them international. This done, the wiry little man drank six more cups of coffee, smoked two further cigars, dictated several 'eyes only' memoranda, and returned to his club at two-thirty a.m. At six-thirty he would be back at his desk with another Napoleon awaiting his first coffee of the day.

Patrick (Paddy) Kennedy could hardly believe his ears. Since being promoted to the Council he had been made privy to a wide variety of things he would never have believed under normal circumstances. But this, this really took the biscuit. He shot an incredulous glance at the weasel of a man who had been assiduously bending his ear for the past ten minutes. He held up his hand.

'Wait a minute, Seamus,' he hissed, careful not to raise his voice. The bar was supposed to be a safe one and they were the only customers but you never could tell these days. 'Are you tryin' to tell me the *English* have sent us a warning?'

Seamus O'Malley nodded his thin, sharp featured head and took a quick gulp of his Guinness. His long, pointed nose gleamed redly. He tweaked it gently between forefinger and thumb.

'Aye, that's right. But 'twas the Americans passed it on.' He glanced about his surreptitiously. 'The English are after sayin' they think something's going on they can't understand. They don't think it was the Prods that killed McEwan and his squad. They think something else is happening but they don't know what it is yet.'

Kennedy, like the ex-boxer he was, shuffled his feet impatiently and made the characteristic shrugging motion of the pugilist. 'They're just tryin' to cover up,' he grunted. 'Quite likely the SAS did them in.'

O'Malley shook his head.

'No, no. Whoever killed them chopped them up. Hands, arms, feet. You know the Brits don't go in for that sort o' thing.' He lowered his voice almost to a whisper. 'They say they cut McEwan's balls off.'

Kennedy's wind-reddened face blanched.

'Well, what the hell are they tellin' us for?'

O'Malley took another healthy swig at his drink. His ferret face was suddenly concerned.

'Well, they figure whoever cut them up did it to get information. One of them, probably all of them, must have talked in the end. They say the place was like a butcher's shop. Now that means these HAWL people likely have a list of names as long as your arm and probably just as many addresses. What the English don't want is you fellows goin' on the rampage out o' revenge. That's why they're tellin' us.'

Paddy Kennedy's face lengthened. He didn't like what he was hearing but he could recognise the possible truth in it. He could also see it was a two-edged thing, neither particularly good for the IRA. If they chose to ignore the warning the English would be given an enormous propaganda weapon. If they accepted the warning and pulled their men out for a while then the same thing would happen. The English would be happy either way and this HAWL would be credited with stopping the Republicans dead in their tracks. He downed the last of his drink. The barman who had remained discreetly at the far end of the bar came up and replenished their drinks.

Paddy waited until he had retreated once more.

'What the hell am I supposed to do about it?'

O'Malley pinched his red beak savagely. 'Warn the Council,' he grimaced. 'Warn the bloody Council. It's all you can do.'

Sadiq Ali Qadar was on the point of emerging from a delicious sleep. Invariably he awakened late when he was in London. This was possibly due to the fact he rarely managed to get to bed before three a.m. at the earliest. Even then it was generally in the company of a woman. Or two. Or sometimes, on an odd occasion, a good-looking boy. Today he was alone. His nubile and satisfyingly acrobatic companion of the night had long since taken her money and departed. That, he supposed, would have been somewhere around seven a.m. They usually liked to be clear of the hotel before it really began to wake up for the business of the day.

Sadiq liked London. He loved the hustle, enjoyed the pomp, and lapped up the entertainment. The clubs were good, the whores surprisingly obliging, and best of all, he felt safe here. He was not wanted by the British police. The fools probably didn't even know him and even if they did he doubted very much if they would do anything save slap his wrist and warn him not to be a bad boy. Sadiq had good reason to thank his foresight in providing himself with a Saudi passport. For some reason he had never been able to understand, the British appeared to have a soft spot for Saudis and allowed them to get away with things other nationalities would not. Possibly it was because they realised the Saudis, despite their money and new modern cities, still retained the tent and camel mentality and, while appearing to advance on the surface, were actually running backwards at a great rate of knots. Still, that wasn't his problem. The Saudis, the most spy-ridden people in the world, would eventually have to work out their own salvation. Meanwhile he was content that to all intents and purposes he was a Saudi national.

Sadiq had originally been a Palestinian. Not, of course, that there really was any such thing any more. Palestine had been gone for forty years. Still, he had been a Palestinian and had served with Arafat. But he had soon learned there was little profit in getting his arse shot at by trigger-happy Israelis who were not about to give up one square inch of territory. There had to be an easier way to keep himself fed and happy and at the same time keep up his undoubted addiction to killing.

The Ayatollah Khomeini had provided this for him by establishing a new cadre of terrorists for the greater promotion of Islam. More correctly, of course, it was for the greater promotion of the Ayatollah and the Shi'ite religious party line. The fact that Sadiq himself was a Sunni did not stop him, nor, for that matter, did it deter the Iranians. His PLO experience was welcomed, money was no object, and he got back to the business he enjoyed most – killing. Sadiq, however, had made it quite clear he had no intention of tackling any suicide missions. He would quite happily slaughter infidels but there was no way he was going to die with them. This was not due to any religious objection on Sadiq's part. He simply enjoyed life too much.

Which was why he was here in London now.

Eight days ago he had successfully introduced a bomb into a Paris school bus. Unfortunately something had gone wrong with the timing device. He supposed he should not have paid so much attention to the IRA instructor, but then it was always easy to be wise after the event. The bomb had exploded *after* the children had disembarked. Not even the driver had been hurt as he had promptly taken off for a nearby café for his morning coffee. The French had not been too happy about the attempt however, and he'd got out of Paris until the heat cooled down a little.

Sadiq really didn't want to get out of bed but he thought he had better. The hotel staff were accustomed to his ways by now. They would not come to clean up the suite until they were sure he was up and about, or, better still, out of the building altogether. He supposed he had better let them get on with it. He yawned, stretched, and flicked open his eyes.

It was then Sadiq realised something was wrong. Of the three disparate actions he had attempted only one worked. His eyes opened.

His mouth was very effectively sealed by something stuffed

into it then held in place by a broad band of surgical tape. His wrists, ankles, legs and upper arms were securely bound by something which bit sharply into his flesh. *Wire*. He did not make the mistake of struggling to free himself. Already he could feel a thin trickle of blood on his wrists, and all he had attempted to do was stretch.

Sadiq's mind raced. Somehow he had been knocked out while he slept, probably by some form of gas. He could remember paying off the little whore, so it must have been done sometime after her departure. This meant that someone was aware of his habits. Therefore it was a professional job. This was also borne out by the use of wire to restrain him.

Professionals!

Sadiq Ali Qadar's immediate reaction was that the Israelis had finally caught up with him. He rejected this almost immediately. He was far too small a fish for them to worry about. Besides, he had not been active with the PLO for over two years. The French then? Maybe the Iraqis? He did not think it could be the French. *They* would probably have asked the British to do the job for them. Anyway he was convinced his tracks were fairly well covered and it would be unlikely they would be on to him so soon. Now, the Iraqis were a possibility. They'd want him simply because he was a Khomeini man. But was their organisation big enough and good enough to track him here? Sadiq did not think so.

Sadiq could not work out with any degree of certainty in whose hands he was held. But he was at least reasonably confident the intention was to kill him immediately, or else why trouble to incapacitate him? Well, where there was life there was a certain degree of hope. Given half a chance he might just get out of this yet.

The door between the bedroom and the small living room of the suite opened. Sadiq's heart sank. Framed in the doorway, like something out of a nightmare, stood a man in a balaclava helmet and a black wet suit. But this man was not dressed for swimming. Nor, for that matter, were the instruments in his hands designed for fishing.

Sadiq Ali Qadar knew, with a sudden cold conviction, that he was about to die.

Chapter Four

The rooming house in Railway Street was perhaps one of the most insalubrious places it had ever been Anne Parkinson's misfortune to encounter. Set almost exactly in the centre of an ancient sandstone tenement it displayed all the signs of imminent disintegration. Walls were chalked and sprayed with obscene graffiti. Most of the green paintwork had long since peeled away, revealing an ugly brown coating beneath, which had also begun to blister, giving coy glimpses of a glaring red and leaving the woodwork with an unsavoury diseased appearance. Several of the windows were broken and roughly covered over with cardboard or plywood. One or two had smaller breaks stuffed with soggy newspaper. There were three steps to the front door and even these had a chipped, cracked, desperate appearance and the battered, peeling door sagged loosely open on rusting, scabrous hinges. The basement, guarded by an equally rusted iron railing, was filled with an ugly miscellany of junk, blown newspapers, cigarette packets, bottles, and dog shit. It stank of mildew and an unholy mixture of urine and rotting food and fruit.

The door, which looked as if it hadn't been closed in years, opened into a long, filthy, poorly lit tunnel smelling of neglect and decay. Worn, litter-covered concrete stairs led to the upper floors from a dismal recess halfway along the tunnel. Two equally dilapidated doors faced into the corridor from left and right. The door on the right bore a crudely painted board on which could be read the word 'caretaker'. From behind it a radio at maximum volume blasted discordant rock music.

Anne Parkinson, her immaculately tailored green two-piece

suit as out of place in those surroundings as a diamond in a dung heap, wrinkled her nose distastefully and knocked on the door labelled 'caretaker'.

Bill Wilkinson's trail had not been hard to follow. She had, quite simply, followed his descent from pub to pub. Beginning with the very pleasant local, she had tracked him carefully through the hostelries he was no longer welcome in. As she did so she noticed how progressively disreputable each successive establishment became. His latest watering hole, the seedy Railway Halt, had been as broken down as its surroundings. The landlord, who looked as if he might be his own best customer, had directed her to this building. There was no answer to her knock.

She banged on the door hard with the edge of her small fist.

Presently, with a great rattling of chains and bolts, the door opened a few inches. Pakistan's answer to Neanderthal Man peered out at her from under beetling brows. Recognising she was a woman and apparently alone, he allowed the door to open a further half inch. The cacaphony of the pop group hammered her ears. The air was suddenly redolent with the odours of cabbage and curry.

'What do you want?'

The Pakistani on the other side of the door, which was still held securely by two stainless steel chains, almost bellowed the words to make himself heard.

'Do you have a William Wilkinson living here?' Anne yelled above the din.

The man behind the door obviously could not hear her. Turning his head he screamed something in Urdu. The volume of the pop group immediately dropped several decibels. Showing a series of black and broken teeth in what Anne charitably took to be an apologetic grin, the Pakistani returned his face to the crack. Anne repeated the question.

The brown-faced cave dweller nodded.

'One up. Number 7.'

The door closed abruptly and was immediately followed by the rattle of bolts being driven home. The pop group swelled to its original mind-jolting volume.

Number 7 proved to be a thin, plywood door which looked

as if it had succumbed several times to kicks from heavy boots. Anne tapped lightly on the surface feeling the plywood buckle slightly under her knuckles. There was no reply. Placing an ear close to the thin panelling she listened carefully. She thought she heard vague, animal sounds from the other side but could not be certain. A trifle warily she tried the handle.

The door was not locked. In fact it was doubtful if it could be locked. It swung shakily open and the thick stench of stale booze and vomit hit her like a hammer. Involuntarily she recoiled slightly from it.

She found herself looking into what purported to be a living-cum-dining room. It contained a sagging, sad-looking easy chair with two rips in the upholstered back, an ancient, stained kitchen table, a paper thin strip of carpeting and nothing else. Nothing, that is, save an accumulated litter of newspapers, carrier bags, old food cartons, beer cans and empty Scotch bottles galore. Here and there an odd article of clothing lay where it had been dropped. The room boasted two windows which bore neither curtain nor blind. Both were broken. One had been boarded off with plywood, the other with a piece of cardboard labelled Heinz. The surviving glass looked as if it had not been cleaned since the house was built. A half dozen cheap, dirty glasses lay on the table, one on its side.

Stepping cautiously over the threshold and striving to ignore the stench Anne peered cautiously about her. She spotted what might be the door to the bedroom. It was slightly ajar. Brushing an empty bottle to one side and unaccountably shivering as it rolled away across bare floorboards. Anne walked towards the door and pushed it open.

Her guess had been correct.

The room contained a rickety wardrobe one door of which hung drunkenly open from a single hinge, and a narrow, metal framed bed. On the bed, sprawled face down across it, one arm trailing limply to the floor, lay Bill Wilkinson. He was still fully dressed except, oddly, for one shoe. His face was a dull, dirty, greyish colour and he had not, as far as Anne could see, shaved for several days. His mouth hung slackly open. A tiny dribble of spit dangled from his lips. Anne had seen enough drunks in her day to know that this one would be a long time before he regained consciousness. She retraced her steps to the scrofulous landing and, carefully closing the rickety door of number 7 behind her, made her way back to the den of the Neanderthal Pakistani.

Mercifully the blare of the pop group had been strangled. She listened to the rattle of the bolts being withdrawn. The door opened its familiar few inches. The Pakistani glowered out at her.

'You are finding him?'

'Yes. Yes, I did, thank you. But he - er - he is in no condition to talk to me at the moment.' Rummaging in her purse Anne produced a small notebook and a ballpoint. She scribbled a second then tore the leaf from the book. The ugly face behind the door watched her impassively. Anne carefully folded a five pound note into the page and, flashing a smile at the face behind the door, held it out. A grubby brown hand snatched it from her.

'When Mr Wilkinson is - er - feeling better perhaps you will be kind enough to telephone me at that number. It's important I talk to him.'

The fiver, by some peculiar feat of Eastern legerdemain, vanished while the Pakistani examined the notebook page. He grunted and nodded his head. 'I phone,' he said, and closed the door.

The demise of Sadiq Ali Qadar was made known to the *Express* in the same manner as had the Roseford massacre. This time the caller asked for Tim Carter by name. Tim, the memory of the blood-spattered room still terribly fresh in his mind, shuddered involuntarily as the flat, emotionless voice spoke in his ear.

'Sadiq Ali Qadar, responsible for the recent attempt to bomb a Paris school bus, guilty of the murder of one unarmed Israeli soldier and four Israeli citizens, and the killing of several Lebanese civilians, can be found in Suite 43 at the Grand Bedford.'

White-faced, Carter took the tape to his editor. Even the hardened veteran was shaken.

'Jeesus Christ!' he exploded. 'What the hell have we got

here? These people have only just done in three terrorists and they're at it again within a few hours.' Tim shudderingly noted the older man had automatically assumed Qadar was dead. The Scot's hard blue eyes bored into those of the investigative reporter. A blunt forefinger stabbed at the younger man. 'I don't know what the hell is going on here but you can take it from me it's *big*. I've got the feeling this is just the beginning. The tip of the bloody iceberg.

'Forget whatever else you're working on. Hand the drug thing over to Simpson. These people seem to have picked you to communicate with so I'm going along with their choice. From now on you'll concentrate on this HAWL thing.'

Carter gawped slightly at his chief.

'Are you telling me you think there's going to be more of this . . . ' – his stomach lurched at the thought – 'this bloody killing?'

The older man glowered at him grimly.

'You're damned right I am, laddie. I don't know the whys and the wherefores of it yet but something very odd is beginning to happen out there and this paper wants to know what it is.' He grinned mirthlessly. 'Now you get over to the Grand Bedford' – he reached for the telephone – 'I'm ringing Special Branch now.'

They found Sadiq Ali Qadar still in bed. Or at least most of him was. Some of him had been tossed carelessly on the floor like so much unwanted garbage. They also found a blood-stained wet suit, a woollen balaclava, a Black and Decker electric drill, a hacksaw, and an ugly, curved bladed cobbler's knife. They found, too, the cheap canvas carry-all in which the killer had presumably carried the wet suit and his grim tools. On the wall of the bedroom, written very neatly with a finger dipped in the unfortunate Sadiq's blood were the letters *HAWL.*

Sir Thomas Griff was scarcely visible behind a thick choking cloud of smoke when his duty secretary brought him his twenty-third cup of coffee. He nodded his thanks to the luckless girl who escaped, red-faced and half-asphyxiated, into the cleaner air of the outer office there to indulge in a five minute coughing bout before returning to her desk. Like all good secretaries she knew her boss was disturbed. His demonic inroads into a new box of Napoleons told her that much. She suspected it had something to do with a telephone call he had received just over two hours ago but she knew better than enquire. Her job at times like these (and there had been many over the years) was to keep an eye on the tiny red bulb placed just to the left of her typewriter. When it glowed, which was often, a fresh cup of coffee was required.

Sir Thomas was indeed disturbed.

As suspected by his secretary the telephone call had been the catalyst precipitating his present condition. It had come from the high ranking police officer he had dined with the previous evening. The call had been a short one informing him of the bloody departure of Sadiq Ali Qadar from the land of the living.

Sir Thomas was not in the least perturbed by the removal of another terrorist from the streets. In fact, if the truth were known, he found their execution rather laudable. However there were implications here which caused him considerable concern. The method of execution had been rather crude to say the least. This, he thought, had been done for two reasons. One: for the purpose of extracting information; and two: to inspire fear.

Both reasons bothered him.

How much information was this HAWL group in possession of? With their methods it would not take too long for them to expand on the knowledge they already had. The way would then be open for them to eventually get to the shadowy leaders of the various groups. If, in fact, that was their ultimate goal.

The fear angle was something else. He was not quite certain what the motivation was here. Could it be that some group aimed to terrify the others into conforming with one common aim? Was this, in fact, the beginnings of a terrorist army with tentacles covering the world?

Sir Thomas stripped the wrapper from yet another Napoleon. Lighting it with a Swan Vestas he tossed the matches carelessly on his desk.

Already there was considerable evidence some of the activist dissident groups were tenuously linked in the matter of arms procurement, training, and even, to some extent, common aims. In a lot of this, of course, the fine hand of the Libyan dictator Gaddafi could be detected but he was no longer alone. There were others, deep in the shadows, who also pulled strings. One of these, and possibly in the end the only manipulator, was undoubtedly Moscow. But were the Russians behind this?

HAWL troubled him too. Who the hell were they, regardless of who pulled their strings? Where had they suddenly appeared from? What precisely were their aims? What did they *really* want? He mulled the letters round in his head for a while striving to put words to the acronym. Finally he gave it up as a bad job. Sooner or later the organisation they represented would make an announcement. They always did. Like actors they *had* to see their name in lights or the game wasn't worth playing.

His mind shot off at a tangent for a moment as he thought of actors. That damned Irish alcoholic Richard Breen had been at it again. Shooting his mouth off to the press about how badly the British were treating the Irish. Seemed to forget that those particular Irish had chosen to be British. Dammit, he'd all but commended the IRA for the Granada Bomb. Obviously the idiot had forgotten that the same people who had been killed were the people who had given him his career. If the bugger weren't such a mediocre actor one could get quite annoyed with him. Obviously he needed all the publicity he could get and violent death usually guaranteed that. God alone knew what the fool would have to say about the Roseford incident.

Shrugging, he turned his mind back to the problem on hand. Just as he had guessed before he really started to think about it, he had little option. This HAWL thing had to be nipped in the bud. And quickly. He allowed his mind to race over the known facts for a moment or two more. He did not turn his people loose easily. Once off the leash the very nature of their work made it difficult, occasionally impossible, to call them off.

With something like a sigh he pulled open the top drawer on the right of his desk and looked for a moment at the green telephone squatting there. Resting his cigar on an overflowing ashtray he picked up the receiver and dialled a two digit number. Couching the receiver between his ear and his shoulder he retrieved his cigar and settled back in his chair listening to the ringing tone. Sometimes it took several minutes before calls made on the green telephone were answered. The twelve men and two women on the other ends of the green line never answered unless they were alone. Sometimes the delay was simply occasioned by the fact they had not noticed the discreet flashing green light which served instead of an audible ring.

His secretary entered quietly with a fresh coffee. Her face tightened slightly at the sight of the green telephone but she made no comment. Retrieving his empty cup she left as silently as she had come. Griff watched her go through a cloud of smoke. The call on the green telephone would never be mentioned. Not even her two colleagues would ever learn of it. All three were aware of the significance of the green line. All had seen it in use. None knew the exact frequency of the calls and none of them wanted to.

Sir Thomas was halfway through his coffee when the connection was finally made. He spoke briskly. 'Can you get over here in the next hour?'

'Yes, sir,' replied Gerald Parkinson and closed the connection.

Chapter Five

There is something about the hour of midnight which has an odd effect upon the Celtic mind. Perhaps it is some hang-over from ancient, long forgotten rites or simply the awakening of childhood tales of ghosties, demons, hobgoblins, and witches. Whatever the cause, it is there, lurking in the back of the mind, waiting to surface when a cloud scuds over the face of the moon and familiar landscapes suddenly become peopled with strange, forbidding shadows. Or perhaps it crouches like a tiny animal to spring to heart-stopping life when rain sheets out of an inky sky and winds create uncertain funereal sounds among the stark boughs of trees stripped naked to meet the small death of winter. Sometimes too it emerges from its lonely corner when the fogs swirl in from the sea and the night is alive with formless, swirling, manacing shapes and shadows reaching and groping blindly for the lonely wayfarer.

Deep, deep in every Celt lurks this grim, nameless dread of things unknown. A tiny lost knot of terror which, for the most part, rarely unravels but remains buried deep in the innermost reaches of the subconscious. Occasionally, when the time is right, the knot springs free.

Seamus O'Malley owned a tiny farm about three miles east of Kildare in County Wicklow. It was not much of a place. Half a dozen fields and a tiny, single storey cottage of the thatched variety described by visiting Americans as 'picturesque' or 'quaint'. Seamus had inherited the place from his father who had worked himself into an early grave striving to extract a meagre living from the soil which had killed his father before him. Seamus, however, had no intention of following the ill fated footsteps of his father and grandfather. There was a living to be made from the land but at best it would have been a bleak and precarious existence. That was not for Seamus.

Years ago Seamus, and others of his ilk, had learned there was money to be made from the Republican movement by obtaining and concealing arms and explosives and by providing 'safe' stop-overs for terrorists on the run. The fact he was quietly milking the same cause he so fervently espoused did not trouble Seamus in the least. In his view there was always money to be made in any war and if it wasn't him then it would be somebody else. Nevertheless he was careful to make his depradations reasonable. Just enough to keep him quietly comfortable and no more. A small but steady supplement to what he could earn from the farm. Greed could bring summary retribution in the form of knee-capping and Seamus didn't have the stomach for that.

Over the years Seamus had gradually grown to a position of some trust and the movement had involved him in other things besides arms. Nothing much, because Seamus was not a fighting man, but he was very useful as a suspicion-free messenger. To Seamus, however, as he carried obscure messages to even more obscure people, it seemed his importance to the movement was growing. In his own mind he saw himself as a vital - no, essential - cog in the machinery. A very important man indeed in the Irish Republican Army.

It was just after midnight and Seamus was walking the three miles from Kildare to his farm. Although he was fairly well-oiled with about a gallon of Guinness and a few whiskies, he was neither drunk nor enjoying the walk. Seamus, in fact, was worrying. And the more he worried the more lonely and exposed he felt.

It was one of those November nights when the sky, palely illumined by a hidden moon, appeared to be nothing more than a low mass of ugly cloud which seemed to constantly swirl and reform itself even as you looked up at it. No, rain, but little patches of damp, cloying mist hung in the dips of the narrow thickly hedged road. There was not much light but just enough to enable Seamus to avoid most of the water-filled potholes littering the road in abundance. Not, of course that you could really call it light at all – just a softening of the gloom which, if he kept his head down, enabled him to discern the inkier patches of the potholes. No perceptible wind but what there was drifted suddenly out of nowhere for long enough to set the hedgerows sighing before vanishing.

Seamus, his trousers tucked into heavy duty rubber boots, listened to the hollow echo of his footsteps, as hands deep in the pockets of his duffel he trudged on. Since he had delivered his message to Paddy Kennedy two days ago he had been very uneasy. The English had to be worried or they would never have done such a thing and if it bothered them then it certainly bothered Seamus O'Malley.

Had he not twice hidden Sean McEwan before they'd finally got him safely across the water? Once for a couple of days but the second time had been for nearly two weeks. If McEwan had talked, and when someone had his balls in one hand and a fuckin' great knife in the other Seamus couldn't see how he could have done otherwise, then it was a safe bet he would have given his torturers *his* name.

A wayward breeze whispered a moment and was gone. Seamus shivered and shrugged deeper into his duffel.

Hell, Seamus thought, he was an important man in the movement. Like as not this HAWL bunch would have his name high on their list. It stood to reason that sooner or later they would be after him. Sweet Jesus, they'd done in that Arab in a big hotel in broad daylight. What chance would he have out here in the middle of nowhere? Somehow he'd have to get out. Simply bugger off and leave the farm. The question was, where could he go where he'd be safe?

From far behind him, lost in the swirl of mist and the darkness, Seamus picked up an instinctive impression of movement. He stopped, half-turned, and peered back the way he had come. He could see nothing and there was no sound out of key with the vague whisperings of the night. But the impression that some living, breathing thing waited back along the road remained with him. He strained into the darkness but all he could see and hear was the vague, unreal swirl of the mist in the diffused, insubstantial light, and the heavy, pumping thud of his own heart.

For several pulsing minutes, Seamus stood motionless in the centre of the narrow road bracing himself to meet the challenge of the unknown something in the darkness. But the challenge did not come. Apart from himself there appeared to be nothing alive in the area. Nothing moved, nothing breathed.

Shrugging silently, but acutely conscious of the hair prickling along the back of his neck, Seamus continued on his plodding way.

Much though he would have liked to put the entire affair out of his mind, Tim Carter's graphic description of the scene at Roseford Farm kept flooding back to haunt him. He could visualise only too well the burly, powerful McEwan nailed to a table and forced to watch his comrades being dismembered with a fire axe. In his mind's eye Seamus could follow the swinging arc of the blade. See it shear through muscle and bone like a knife through butter. Witness the great gout of dark blood, hear the agonised screaming of the victim, and watch Tom Flynn's severed hand, fingers still clawing convulsively, leap away from the gaping stump of his wrist.

In spite of himself Seamus felt his right wrist twinge sympathetically. He clenched his fist deep in his pocket. Jesus, but with the Arab they'd used a hacksaw! Flinching in the darkness, he fought to keep the terrible gory images from his mind.

Something scrunched lightly on the road behind him.

Seamus's heart took a sickening leap. He halted in mid-stride. Involuntarily his hands leaped from his pockets, his head drew low on his neck, his shoulders hunched protectively. He braced himself for the impact of whatever.

A fleeting split second later, when his brain had recorded nothing striking his body, Seamus was running. Fleeing clumsily along the dark road, heedless of potholes or banks of mist. Racing in blind, unseeing terror from the unspeakable horror behind him. Several times, clumsy in his rubber boots, he fell sprawling on the wet and broken macadam, but each time, sobbing, almost choking on his fear, he was on his feet instantly and impervious to bruises and cuts running madly on.

The lights of his cottage loomed suddenly ahead.

Blessing himself for his habit of leaving the lights burning and the door unlatched Seamus hurled himself into the warmth and brightness of his living room. Eyes glittering with a manic glare, he slammed the door behind him and rammed home the two heavy bolts which secured it. Gasping, dragging great gulps of air into tortured lungs, he lunged for the double-barrelled Purdy hanging above the fireplace. Frantic eyes never leaving the door or the two small windows he broke the gun and, fumbling in an ancient dresser drawer, found two O-gauge cartridges and rammed them into the breach.

By Jesus, they weren't going to get him! He was ready for them. Let them come. Just let them come.

Like all cottages of its type the door opened directly into the main room of the building. From here a door on either side opened into what had originally been bedrooms. When Seamus was a boy the room he now crouched in like an animal at bay, had been the kitchen and living room. O'Malley, with some of the money he had garnered from the Republicans had, years ago, converted the larger of the two bedrooms, dividing it into a compact kitchen and bathroom. The kitchen was accessible directly from the room he stood in while the bathroom and toilet were only available via the kitchen. Inconvenient perhaps, but damned sight better than the old outside privy and zinc bath in front of the kitchen fire. There was no other way in or out of the cottage apart from the stout barred door. It had long been Seamus's intention to install a rear entrance. He now thanked his maker he had never got round to it.

Weasel face chalk white, long, pointed nose pinched tightly at the nostrils, button eyes glaring wildly at the door, Seamus crouched by the comforting bulk of the dresser and listened to the harsh sound of his own breathing rasping in the still warm air.

They were coming for him. The bastards were out there somewhere trying to find a way to get at him. Well, they weren't going to cut up Seamus O'Malley. No, by God they weren't. Nobody was going to cut his balls off. The first thing that moved out there was getting it. Both barrels. They wouldn't get close enough to hack him to bits.

The unmistakeable sound of a soft footfall.

Seamus whirled. Holy Mother of God, they were in the kitchen!

He snapped the comforting butt of the Purdy into his shoulder. The connecting door was yanked unceremoniously open. Seamus squeezed both triggers. The heavy boom of the Purdy dinned in the room like the roar of a cannon.

In the same instant his finger tightened on the triggers, Seamus O'Malley recognised the broken-nosed grinning face of Paddy Kennedy. Then the familiar face distintegrated into a splashing red-grey mush and the square, trim body of the ex-boxer was lifted off its feet and hurled back into the kitchen.

Chapter Six

Anne Parkinson had started to put together the framework of her story and she was saddened by it.

Because of the notoriety of the Granada Bomb incident she had taken that as a starting point. Now, only beginning to grope her way into the hidden effects of terror attacks upon the innocent, she was finding she was stumbling blindly into a sea of tragedy, despair, and tears. The initial shocked brave words for the media were long gone. Now there was a tight-lipped anger, a sense of bewildered impotence and a general feeling that nobody cared.

As one unfortunate victim learning to walk on an artificial leg told her: 'People just don't care any more. There's a lot more fuss made over injured horses than there is over people like us. Just read your newspapers. They never say anything about children losing limbs or being scarred for life. Never mention women and men losing their livelihoods because of what has happened to them. We're news for a day . . . maybe not even that . . . then we're replaced by some doctor having it away with one of his patients, or a film star cutting his finger while playing shove-halfpenny. As a rule, the most that's ever said is that so many were killed or injured. After that we're forgotten.

'What the hell do you people think happens to a mother who sees her child blown to bits, or to a man who learns he can never be a father or even work again? How do you think they feel when, on the odd occasion they manage to catch some of these maniacs, all they do is lock them up for a few years? Do you think it makes them happy?'

Anne's answer to this had sounded hollow, even to herself. 'Perhaps,' she suggested, 'the Government simply doesn't want to give the terrorists too much publicity. Maybe they just don't want to foster any kind of panic by giving too much detail.'

The fifty-two year old cripple looked at her disbelievingly. His voice suddenly had an icy edge to it: 'Panic, Miss Parkinson? If you're talking about the United States, perhaps. But this is Britain. We're a part of Europe. Dammit, what more do we need to learn about bombs in this part of the world? Europe contains the world's experts on being bombed. No, Miss, it's got nothing to do with panic. It's because we no longer care. It's become commonplace – a part of the European way of life. We simply absorb it, thank our lucky stars it wasn't us, and carry on.'

In spite of herself Anne was forced to admit he had a point. Nor was he alone in expressing it. Anne was particularly shocked by his and other people's reactions to the HAWL massacre at Roseford Farm. The cripple's eyes positively gleamed with delight.

'HAWL, Miss? I'll tell you what I think of them. I hope there's bloody hundreds of them out there. Every time I strap on this damned leg of mine I thank God they're giving the terrorists a taste of what I got. Long may they reign, I say. And if they're looking for volunteers they can have me any time – for what I'm worth,' he added bitterly.

Later, when she had related this attitude to her brother, his green eyes, so like her own, had suddenly become thoughtful.

'You say this attitude is pretty general, Anne?'

She was momentarily flustered by his apparent seriousness.

'Well, I've only just got started, you know. I mean, I haven't been to Ireland or anywhere else yet. But yes, I'd say it's pretty general among the few I've talked to.' She shivered slightly. 'One woman I talked to – her baby was blown out of his pram and suffered terrible brain damage – actually quite frightened me. I've never met anyone so full of hate. I'm certain she would have happily cut up those terrorists all by herself. The way she talked, McEwan's squad got off very lightly.' She glanced at her brother curiously. 'Why are you so interested all of a sudden, Gerry?'

He grinned disarmingly.

'Hell, it's really you I'm interested in, Anne. Now that you've become a famous TV personality type I'm curious to see how you go about your work. I mean, it's all very different to what us staid Civil Service types are used to.' He laughed infectiously. 'You didn't tell me how you got on with your homing pigeon drunk last night.'

Anne giggled. 'A bit of a let down, really. When the caretaker phoned he carefully forgot to tell me Wilkinson was already half drunk when he left. When I caught up with him at the pub all I could manage to get out of him were monosyllabic grunts while he drank himself unconscious – at my expense.' She giggled again. 'What's more it cost me a fiver to get two of the local rough necks to carry him home.'

Her brother laughed. 'Not what you would call a productive evening then?'

She shook her auburn head. 'No, it wasn't. But I'll keep after him though. There's a story in that pathetic man and I'm going to get it before I'm very much older.'

John Lindsay Hughes, folded into a corner on the nine-fifteen from Ewell, looked exactly what he was: a gangling, middle-aged academic peering uncertainly through black-framed spectacles at a world he could not understand. Yesterday, at this same time, he had been happily enfolded in the booklined bosom of his Cambridge rooms. Today, because of a chance encounter with the *Express*, he was on his way to meet a man he had never heard of.

His accidental encounter with the *Express* came as a result of a quick visit from one of his students to discuss an obscure passage in an even obscurer Russian novel. The student, his curiosity satisfied, had departed leaving his copy of the newspaper behind him. With roughly an hour to kill before his first lecture the academic had idly picked it up. While Hughes agreed generally with the newspaper's politics, he was not particularly enamoured of the manner in which they were presented. It was rare, therefore, that he saw it, or bothered to read it. That morning, however, he had found himself rivetted by one of Tim Carter's pieces on the terrorist murders. Four times in all he read the piece before tossing the newspaper to one side and prowling abstractedly along his tightly packed bookshelves. Finally, he selected a fairly modern volume and leafed quickly through it with the expertise born of complete familiarity.

In a moment, grunting with satisfaction, he found the reference he wanted. Studying it for a second he snapped the book shut and squeezed it back into place on the shelves. Slowly, as if he were not quite certain he was doing the right thing, he crossed to the telephone and dialled the *Express* number.

His conversation with Tim Carter had been brief. Very brief. Mainly because he did not have a great deal to say. But apparently what little he did say aroused some interest because within fifteen minutes he was called back to the telephone.

On this occasion he found himself listening to the voice of someone called Sir Thomas Griff. The result of that brief, somewhat one-sided conversation had been his travelling down to his sister's rather pleasant little house in Ewell and spending the night there before taking this train to meet with Sir Thomas.

It was all very perplexing really. After all, it was such a simple thing. He really could not understand what all the fuss was about. There had been absolutely no need to drag him all the way down here. After all, he'd said all he needed to say on the telephone. But Griff had been so damned insistent. Simply would not accept no as an answer. Staring blankly through the window he wondered vaguely who the man was and what had excited his interest so much. Then, finding no easy answers, he turned his attention to the *Telegraph* crossword.

Sir Thomas Griff, when the scholarly Hughes was rather belatedly ushered into his office, was, as usual, behind his desk, half-hidden by a cloud of cigar smoke. Hughes thought the wiry little man reminded him vaguely of a garden gnome. This illusion was quickly dispelled when the little man propelled himself round his desk and shook his visitor's hand warmly. The pedant found himself looking into a pair of brilliant blue eyes which mirrored the enormous intellect lying behind them. Their impact was almost physical. Combined with an overlarge hooked nose and a crest of tousled iron grey hair, those eyes gave his host an almost predatory appearance. Somehow, like a genie from a bottle, Griff appeared to grow in stature as he ushered his visitor into a chair and offered him a cup of coffee. The knight seemed oddly disappointed when Hughes refused. As he retreated behind his desk and picked up his cigar the scholar gained the impression he had been found wanting.

'Now then, Mr – er Professor Hughes. Just what was this you were telling me on the telephone?' Griff's voice was deep, slightly husky, and oddly melodic. Hughes found himself wondering if the little man was Welsh or from one of the Scottish Islands. 'You were saying you believe the letters HAWL are, in fact, a word, and not an acronym. An Arabic word, I believe you said.'

Hughes cleared his throat. 'Er – yes, yes that is so.'

The piercing eyes fixed themselves on the academic's face through the smoke haze. 'Explain please, Professor. How did you arrive at this conclusion?'

Again the lanky Professor cleared his throat. He coughed slightly. The little man was immediately apologetic. 'Oh dear, how very remiss of me.' He glanced at the half-smoked cigar between his fingers. 'Is my smoking bothering you, Professor?'

'No. No, not at all,' protested Hughes. 'In fact I frequently enjoy a good cigar myself.'

The little man was round the desk instantly and proffering a box. Hughes accepted one of the olive green Napoleons with a smile of thanks. He had the feeling he had just redeemed himself in Griff's eyes.

'You'll enjoy that,' said Griff chattily as he moved behind his desk once more. 'Friend of mine over at the American Embassy brings them in for me.' He winked. 'Diplomatic bag, you know. None of this Import Duty business. Only reason I would ever consider emigrating to the States are those cigars.' He waited, beaming companionably, until Hughes had his cigar burning nicely. 'Now, what gives you the idea this is a word?'

Hughes added his contribution to the swirl of smoke in the room. He settled his lanky frame more comfortably in his chair.

'Well, Sir Thomas, as you probably know my subject is languages. One of those languages happens to be Arabic.' The little man behind the desk nodded encouragingly. 'When I glanced through the *Express* yesterday the word, in fact, seemed to almost leap at me. It fitted so well with the subject matter you see.'

Griff leaned forward across his desk.

'I'm not quite sure I follow you there, Professor.'

Hughes puffed contentedly at his cigar.

'The word, Sir Thomas, is *hawl*' – he pronounced it *ho-wull* – 'Translated it means, quite simply, terror.' He warmed to his subject and gestured slightly with his cigar. 'Of course, the Arabs have another word which basically means the same thing. This word is *rouab*. Both words are used in different contexts. For example, the word *hawl* would normally be used in connection with fear of natural events, lightning storms, volcanic eruptions, that sort of thing. *Rouab*, on the other hand, would be used when speaking of the effects of terrorism.'

Griff momentarily forgot his cigar. His blue eyes seemed to blaze through the drifting smoke.

'In that case, Professor, I can't follow your logic. Surely if these people are going to use an Arabic word then the obvious choice would have to be . . . ' – he stumbled slightly on the pronunciation – ' . . . *rouab* and not *hawl*.'

Hughes shook his head slightly. 'Not so. I think there is a very clear distinction here.' He blinked through his heavy spectacles. 'I believe they are using the word as a dedication and as a warning.' He shrugged slightly. 'You may, of course, find other Arabists who would disagree with me, but what I believe is being intimated here is that this form of terror attack is a *natural* reaction to the other. First principles, Sir Thomas. Every action has a *natural* reaction. To put it bluntly, I believe these people are declaring to all terrorist groups that actions taken by them will be met by its equal . . . or worse.'

'Good Christ,' exploded Griff. The melodic resonance was gone from his voice. 'Are you telling me that these people are setting out to terrorise terrorists?'

John Lindsay Hughes smiled beatifically and nodded. 'That, Sir Thomas, is precisely what I am telling you.'

Chapter Seven

Terence O'Mannion, fifty-one year old bachelor and ex-Irish International soccer star, was troubled, but far from desperately so, by the HAWL massacre of the Roseford squad. It was his considered opinion that the English had finally uncovered them and simply wiped them out. The possibility of the killings having been perpetrated by some outside agency never even entered his head. Who else but the bloody British could possibly want to harm the IRA? It was nothing more than a propaganda trick to scare them into cutting back or maybe even stop their attacks for a while. If the English thought they were stupid enough to fall for such a transparent trick then more fool them.

What did trouble O'Mannion, however, was the effect upon the rank and file. Not, of course, that he believed for one moment the men were cowards or easily frightened. But the concept of an unknown, unseen enemy killing in such a horrible manner was not having a good effect upon morale. That idiot Seamus O'Malley blowing the head off Paddy Kennedy had been no help. Only proved how nervous the men in the field were becoming. Not, of course, that O'Malley could ever have been classed as a fighting man. Besides, he was dead now anyway – O'Rourke had seen to that! Still, it was unsettling. The Council, while voting unanimously to continue the struggle, had not played down the fact that perhaps the English could be right. They had advocated extra care – just in case.

O'Mannion, who had himself seen considerable action over the years and cheerfully claimed responsibility for the killing of an unarmed off-duty policeman at the door of his own home and in the presence of his wife and children, did not see the lethal irony in the situation. Would not, in any case, have understood had it been explained to him in the most simple terms. The fact that somebody was doing to them what they had been doing to their own people for years was completely lost upon him. He had other things on his mind besides HAWL.

The organisation was desperately short of cash. The ever rising cost of killing was beginning to weaken them. Two ransom attacks had failed miserably, Noraid funds had been reduced to a trickle, they were perilously close to being broke. Maybe they could raise a bit through Bank raids in the Republic but the Garda would be on the lookout for that. They could lose a few more men, and they didn't have all that many of them to spare.

As if that wasn't enough they had the escapees from the Maze on their hands. Getting them out of the country took a hell of a lot of money as well. Just getting them across the water into England and setting them up there cost a fair bit on its own and strange Irish men were not exactly welcomed with open arms any more. And the Continent was more expensive still. Jesus, they were talking about plastic surgery and all that crap. Did they have the faintest idea what all that would cost? Sure, the Maze breakout had been grand publicity but the end cost was going to be astronomical and they had to find the money somewhere.

O'Mannion, living comfortably in digs with an obliging landlady just outside Carrickfergus, was also not particularly enamoured of these occasional trips over the border to Council meetings. Even in the South, support for the IRA was dwindling rapidly. Moving around in Dublin could be bloody hazardous on occasions. Not, of course, that his face was all that well known but there was always the chance someone might recognise him and there were not all that many places he knew of he could run to in case of trouble. In the North of course it was a different matter. He knew most of the safe houses there.

Hunching down into the upturned collar of his raincoat as

protection against the fine drizzle he turned into a narrow, dimly lit street which would lead directly to the George Hotel. He'd have a couple of quick drinks in the bar and then turn in for the night. He would need his wits about him tomorrow when he tackled the trip North again.

Sean Carey and Moira McLeary were not particularly concerned with the light drizzle. Like all young people they were more concerned with the immediacy of their own needs and desires. Adverse weather was of secondary importance. Sean and Moira, both first year students at the University, had met at the disco and were strongly attracted to each other. Sean, his eye as always on the main chance, was walking Moira back to her digs.

Moira, a normal, warm-blooded young woman was therefore not particularly concerned when the tall young student wheeled her, not too subtly, into a Stygian side street. Huddling into a handy doorway Moira discovered she could hardly see Sean's face as they entered into their first, experimental kiss. The experiment apparently was a great success because they immediately entered into a protracted, rustling, groping clinch. They were oblivious to draughts, cold hands, and the continuing drizzle.

Presently Moira, gasping and sighing a little, came up for air. Her eyes, still misted with passion, took a few seconds adjusting to the darkness as she gazed blankly over Sean's shoulder.

She screamed.

The shrill, petrifying sound echoed down the dark canyon of the street carrying with it blood chilling undertones of pure terror. Her slim body convulsing and jerking with the effort she screamed again and again.

Sean, all thought of immediate seduction burned from his mind, shied away from her like a startled horse and spun to face the direction of her outflung arm.

At first he thought it was shadow. Then, as his eyes strained into the darkness, the shadow solidified and took a hard, definite shape. He became aware of the raincoated body of Terence O'Mannion swaying gently as it hung by the neck from the crossarm of an unlit lamppost. Pinned to

O'Mannion's raincoat was what appeared to be a placard of some kind. Sean did not attempt to read it. Grabbing the hysterical Moira's ice-cold hand and dragging her stumbling behind him, he fled in search of a Garda.

Some two hours later, when the Garda had finished questioning Moira and Sean and they were being driven to their respective quarters, Kevan Riordan, another member of the Council, was dying horribly in the garage of his neat, but isolated little bungalow. Inside the bungalow, mercifully unaware of what was happening in the garage, Riordan's wife and two children slept in deep, drugged slumber. Riordan himself had been plucked from the bed he shared with his wife and dragged unceremoniously to his place of execution.

Riordan emerged from his gas-induced sleep attempting to scream in agony at the white hot pain searing up his legs. He could only scream inside his head, however, because he was firmly gagged. Nor was he able to see his torturer properly through the agonised tears streaming from his eyes. He did know, however, that he was lashed securely over the bonnet of his car and that someone was using a power drill on his kneecaps.

All in all, it took Kevan Riordan fifteen minutes to die, most of the time in silent, screaming agony. There was little respite given him. Nor were there any questions asked. The hazy, black clad figure of his murderer had gone about his business in dedicated silence. The only sounds apparent in the confines of the garage were the whirr of the power drill and, after a few moments, the dull, biting rasp of a hacksaw through bone.

Riordan died when the first letter of *HAWL* was burned on his chest with an electric soldering iron. He was found by his shrieking, hysterical wife at 8.15 a.m., following a telephone call from the local Garda who had been alerted by the *Express*. Riordan had been castrated. One leg, just below the knee, had been sawn off, as had one arm. Both eyes had been gouged out and he had been knee-capped with his own drill.

Much later that same day two meetings took place. Both were in London. Both were completely unobserved. And both concerned exactly the same subject. None of the participants in either meeting was aware of the other.

A third meeting took place in the smoke-filled office of Sir Thomas Griff.

Sir Thomas, having been informed of the removal of two suspected members of the IRA Inner Council and the killing of a third at the hands of one of their own men, was now very concerned indeed. He had already briefed his visitor on the suspicions of the Cambridge linguist but he was even more troubled by the fact that HAWL, whoever, or whatever they stood for, were in strong danger of being deified by the British Press with the *Express* well out in front as chief worshipper.

'TERROR STRIKES IRA' boomed its headlines and the lead story left its millions of readers in no doubt that HAWL, in spite of its methods, had the backing of the great newspaper.

'Now,' its lead article declared, 'the terrorists who have been responsible for the killing and maiming of hundreds of our citizens over the years, are being given a taste of their own medicine. Perhaps the methods used by HAWL are extreme but they are, at least, discriminate. Innocent bystanders are not being hurt. The war of terror is being taken direct to the enemy with no apparent danger to the general public.

'This newspaper cannot help but wonder how these hardened killers are reacting to the knowledge they are being hunted down by others more implacable and ruthless than themselves. To them, the enemy is no longer the recognisable uniforms of the British army or the Ulster Constabulary. Nor is their punishment any longer confined to a term of imprisonment. Today they have an enemy they cannot recognise, who does not declare himself by conspicuous uniforms. Today they are being watched, stalked and ruthlessly killed. Their deaths, like so many of their own victims, are neither swift nor painless. How must it feel to live with the same fear they themselves created?'

Gerald Parkinson grinned amiably at his chief and tossed the newspaper carelessly on the little man's desk. His green eyes gleamed with sardonic amusement.

'Not much doubt about whose side they're on, sir.'

The little man indicated a pile of newspapers at the side of his desk.

'Yes, but they are not alone. Almost every one of those papers leans sympathetically towards HAWL.' His small, almost feminine hands, stripped the wrapper from yet another Napoleon. 'It's beginning to bother me, Gerald. If those people keep going they are going to have millions of allies out there who would be happy to help them out if things got rough. But what is even worse is the danger that impressionable idiots might try to emulate HAWL. Then where will we be? It hardly bears thinking about.

'Can you imagine it? Before too long perfectly law-abiding citizens might be lynching other law-abiding citizens because they happen to have different accents or colour. Because they *might* be terrorists.'

Parkinson grunted and ran his fingers through his brown hair. 'Odd you should say that, Sir. Anne was virtually telling me the same thing a couple of days ago.'

The little man, his cigar going like the smokestack of an old steam locomotive, leaned forward with interest. Sir Thomas had a very healthy respect for the manner in which the media could influence the public at large. He also held considerable admiration for the undoubted tenacity of their investigative reporters. In the past he had found it beneficial to play along rather than attempt to muzzle them with a D notice.

'Really?' he said. 'Tell me about it.'

Parkinson, himself a non-smoker, did his best to ignore his chief's cigar. Crossing his immaculately trousered legs he briefly recounted Anne's findings among the victims she had spoken to. The little man heard him through in grim silence.

'Yes,' he agreed presently. 'More or less bears out what I've just been saying. But it's not the real worry about all this. HAWL must have some sort of aim. They're trying to get to something, I think. I can't bring myself to believe for one moment that their aim is simply to slaughter the men who lay the bombs or shoot from ambush. With their methods they are gathering information very fast and I'm certain they intend to use it. I think they intend to go after the leaders. Nail the men behind the terrorists. Witness how fast they got to the IRA Inner Council.'

Parkinson said nothing. The little man continued.

'I don't think I have to tell you, Gerald, that a lot of this terrorism is Moscow-inspired and financed. It makes nice propaganda for them. You know the sort of thing – exploited workers fighting to be free of their capitalist oppressors. Also, it keeps the West in a continuous state of unrest. Keeps our minds off what's really happening.' He blew a stream of smoke towards the ceiling. 'Also, of course, the CIA don't exactly have clean hands either. *They* are not above fostering a lot of this and certainly, when it suits them, they don't do damned much to discourage it.

'Following the big boys come the B teams. The Israelis, the PLO, the IRA, ETA, Gadaffi, Khomeini,, BOSS, SWAPO and all the rest of the bunch who're staining the world with their murderous activities. What happens if HAWL goes after the leaders of that merry little crew?'

Parkinson expelled his breath in a long, slow whistle. He did not require a picture painted for him. He could see only too well what his boss was driving at.

'You don't seriously believe that is their eventual aim, sir?'

Griff puffed thoughtfully at his cigar.

'I don't know, Gerald. I honestly don't know. But one thing I *am* sure about. They have to be stopped – permanently – before we find out too late. Now, how did you go on with the lists of the Granada Bomb victims? Any luck?'

The big man leaned forward slightly.

'Well, sir, as you know we fed the names into our various computer systems. Income Tax, Armed Services, National Insurance, Police Records, all that sort of thing and we've come up with a list of about thirty possibles. This is thirty people who seem to have the training and the know-how to be ripe for recruitment to HAWL. Two of them are known mercenaries. I propose to get to them first, then work my way down through the list in order of merit.'

Sir Thomas nodded. His fierce blue eyes were suddenly grave.

'Well, don't waste time, Gerald. I have the feeling we don't have too much to spare.'

Chapter Eight

Anne Parkinson had finally caught up with Bill Wilkinson. In exchange for another fiver the avaricious Pakistani caretaker had agreed to telephone her when Wilkinson appeared sober enough to talk to. The man had not been over confident of her chances.

'Wilkinson *always* drunk,' he snickered. 'He is not a good sober man like Muslim.'

Anne had thought of the many drunken Muslims she had seen around Earls Court and in the West End but held her peace. The proffered fiver vanished with the same bewildering dexterity as its predecessor. Tonight her ten-pound investment had paid off. When her informant rang Anne's first enquiry was as to the sobriety of the former Project Engineer. The voice at the other end had sounded quite huffed.

'Wilkinson is not drunk. He goes to the pub now. Will get drunk soon.'

She had found him at the bar of the Railway Halt. He was trying to wheedle another drink from the bloated publican on the strength of his next Social Security cheque. 'Oh, come on, Cecil,' he said, as she pushed through the swing doors, 'I haven't got too much on the slate – you know I'm good for it.'

The huge man behind the bar, whose veined and mottled complexion betrayed a great fondness for his own stock, glanced up as Anne entered the bar. His heavy jowls wobbled and his tight mouth creased into what Anne charitably thought was intended to be a smile of welcome. He turned away from the pleading Wilkinson.

'Evening, Miss. What would you like?'

It was early yet. Anne and Wilkinson, aside from the gargantuan landlord, were the only people in the bar. Anne shot a quick glance at the former engineer.

He *did* appear to be sober, had even managed to have a shave although his drawn face was nicked in several places. She noticed he was wearing the same slacks and blazer she had seen him in last time. His shirt looked as if he had not taken it off in days. He had exerted some effort and combed his long fair hair and Anne was surprised to observe that were it not for the gaunt, haunted look about him, he was quite good looking. Although he was huddled into his clothes Anne could see he must have been a fit and athletic man. Right now though his hands were trembling violently as he clutched an empty shot glass. It seemed that it was only sheer will power that was holding him up. With a sudden frightening clarity Anne realised she was looking at a man intent on drinking himself to death. She made the landlord's day by flashing him a sample of the smile which had begun to make her a household name in America.

'I'll have a gin and tonic, please. And give Mr Wilkinson a Scotch, will you?'

Wilkinson, hearing his name mentioned, turned his head slightly. Pale, bloodshot grey eyes looked at her from deeply shadowed sockets. For a moment it appeared he was about to speak then the dull, lustreless eyes slid away as the landlord plonked a shot glass on the chipped and scarred mahogany before him.

Murmuring her thanks Anne accepted her own drink but continued to watch Wilkinson with a fascinated aversion. The palsied hands appeared to increase their rate of tremble until they were almost jerking spasmodically. Then the whole man appeared to tense and stiffen as if he were exerting enormous will power. The hands steadied momentarily and swooped like twin birds of prey on the small shot glass. He managed to get the drink to his mouth before the trembling began again. Some of the contents spilled over his chin but he managed to swallow most of it. Anne felt almost sick at the ugly, gloating, greedy expression which flickered across his face as the spirit burned in his stomach.

For a long moment Wilkinson was still. Then he lowered the empty glass to the bar and wiped his chin with the back of a trembling hand. The barman, a strange expression on his face as if he were perhaps seeing an image of himself in a few years to come, picked up the glass and glanced questioningly at the young woman. She nodded curtly not trusting herself to speak. It was not until after he had downed his third drink that Bill Wilkinson decided to acknowledge her presence. Anne had yet to sample her own drink.

'Why are you buying me drinks, Miss?'

His words had the rounded tones of an educated man but his voice had a slight husky timbre to it, put there, she had no doubt, by the prodigious amount of alcohol he consumed. There was also, she noticed, a slight but obvious hard edge which gave her the feeling that Bill Wilkinson, drunk or sober, would not take kindly to strangers probing into his private life. She evaded the question for a moment by sipping at her gin and tonic. With no immediate answer forthcoming, Wilkinson appeared to forget his query and turned his attention back to the hovering landlord. The big man behind the bar, confident his money was safe, now had no hesitation in filling the drunk's glass. What was it to him if the silly bastard didn't know a good thing when he saw it? Christ, if a woman like this came looking for *him* he could think of other things to be doing instead of guzzling scotch like there was going to be no tomorrow.

A few drinks later, when the urgency of his need had apparently been slowed and the trembling had stopped, Wilkinson continued drinking steadily but entered into a stumbling conversation with his good fairy. Under Anne's gentle probing he talked about Nigeria, his service days, his boyhood and his parents and many other things, but never once did he touch upon the subject of his wife and daughter. It was almost as if a section of his mind had been completely shut off and nothing would be allowed to reopen it. Not even this lovely, self-confident, charming woman who kept buying him drinks.

But Anne Parkinson did not mind. As they talked she was beginning to build a picture of what the original whole man had been like: athletic, tough, single-minded to a degree. The complete man's man, yet with a hidden warmth and understanding that would always enable him to see the other person's point of view. He was, she thought, a man with an enormous capacity to love.

When the landlord finally, and regretfully, called time Wilkinson was quite drunk but just capable of standing on his own two feet. Anne, who, apart from her initial gin, had drunk nothing but tonic water, drove him to the door of the decrepit building he lived in. There, before he left the car, she made a date to call for him two days later on Friday, when, she said, they would have a quiet meal and a few drinks together. She was certain the message sunk into his drink-sodden mind because he repeated the day to himself several times as he struggled out of the car. For some reason she could not understand Anne pressed a ten-pound note into his hand before she drove off, leaving him swaying drunkenly on the pavement.

Anne, as she swung the little car into the main stream of traffic, was well satisfied. Wilkinson sober was an articulate intelligent man. What she had to do now was work at gaining his confidence. Sooner or later he would relax enough to open the door in his mind and tell her what she wanted to know. It did not strike her as odd that she was already looking forward to seeing him again. Nor did she find it strange that she had begun to scheme as to how best to get some food into him because he obviously was not doing much eating.

Ken Williamson, listed by the computers as having almost lost his only daughter in the Granada Bomb explosion and noted as being a mercenary and a possible candidate for HAWL, was very definitely off the list. There was, in fact, no possible way he could have been involved in the HAWL killings. This was due to the fact that he had not been in the country for almost three months and because he had been shot through the shoulder in South West Africa two weeks ago. He was currently resident in a South African Hospital.

Gerald Parkinson discovered this five minutes after meeting Williamson's wife. Mrs Williamson, a small plumpish, bird-like woman who reminded Parkinson of a near demented sparrow he had once seen in a cage, met him white-faced and wringing her hands at the door of the little Watford cottage. When he had asked if her husband was at home he thought for an uncertain moment that the little woman was going to faint. She recovered quickly however, and swinging the door wide, invited him in.

Presently he was seated in a comfortable but slightly over-furnished living room, balancing a cup and saucer on his knee and listening to the little woman chatter on about her husband.

'This is the third time in six years Ken has been wounded, you know.' Her faded hazel eyes looked faintly apologetic. 'It's – it's his work, you know. He never could really settle after he left the army. Kept on and on about fighting being the only trade he knew and why shouldn't he be able to make a decent living at it.

'Anyway he finally became a mercenary about eight years ago and did a spell in Oman. Since then he's been all over the place. I only have him home three or four times a year and then only for a week or, at the most, a fortnight.'

She sipped her tea delicately. 'People don't really understand about mercenaries, you know. Everybody seems to think they're hired killers. But that's not true. They're simply soldiers being paid to do the job they have been trained for. An awful lot of nonsense was written about them during the Congo business and now they are stuck with something they don't really deserve. If the press gave as much coverage to terrorism as they do mercs perhaps there wouldn't be quite so much of *that* going on. Mercs are a lot different from terrorists – although you wouldn't think so from some of the rubbish you read in reports. Mercs are soldiers who fight for money and *all* soldiers get paid. I mean, we don't look at the Ghurkas as being mercenaries, do we? Yet that is precisely what they are.'

Parkinson let the little woman babble on. She had obviously been through this justification speech many times before. It had probably become second nature to her and satisfied some hidden pathological need. In a moment or two she appeared to change direction slightly.

'You know, this is Ken's last job, Mr Parkinson. He's

packing it all in when he finishes his tour. Going to retire and grow roses, he says. That's why it's a bit of a shock when strangers like yourself come to the door. I mean, I know his wound isn't serious but you never know out in those foreign countries. You always seem to think the worst. Every time a stranger knocks on the door I just can't help worrying.' She smiled weakly. 'I should be used to it by now, really. I mean, you're the second gentleman to come looking for him today.'

Gerald Parkinson was immediately alert. Tiny warning bells were chiming at the back of his head. 'You say someone else has been here, Mrs Williamson?'

She nodded brightly. 'Oh yes.' She glanced at the clock ticking quietly on the mantle. 'He came about three hours ago. Just asked where Ken could be contacted and when I told him Ken was in South Africa he wanted to know how long he had been there. Seemed quite happy when he learned Ken had been away nearly three months. Didn't even wait for a cup of tea. Just thanked me and left. Quite a nice man he was.'

Parkinson leaned forward in his chair. 'Did this man say WHY he was looking for your husband, Mrs Williamson?'

'Yes, he did. He said he had a job for him but I soon put a stop to that. Told him in no uncertain terms that Ken was retiring. That this was his last job.'

'You thought he was a military man then?'

She glanced at him curiously. 'Yes. Yes I did as a matter of fact. He was tall and very erect and had a sort of authority about him, if you know what I mean. As if he was used to ordering people about.'

'Is there anything else you can remember about him, Mrs Williamson? For example, did he have any kind of accent, or was there anything particularly noticeable about him?'

The little housewife's tired eyes widened with alarm. She sat bolt upright in her chair like a pouter pigeon preparing to defend the nest.

'Why are you so interested, Mr Parkinson? Is my Ken in some kind of trouble?'

He hastened to reassure her. 'No, no, Mrs Williamson. There's nothing at all for you to worry about. Your husband's not in any kind of trouble whatsoever. Please take my word for it. Now, please try to remember, did this other man have an accent or did anything strike you as being a bit odd about him?'

Her worried eyes studied his hard, handsome features for a long moment. She was obviously troubled and he guessed she was trying to make up her mind as to whether she should believe him. She sighed and relaxed slightly.

'Well,' she said thoughtfully. 'Now you come to mention it he DID have a bit of an accent. Foreign like. Not much of a one, but it was there.'

Under his skilful questioning he discovered the unknown visitor had been about six-foot tall, fairly broad-shouldered, was very smartly dressed and wore a fawn British Warm. No, he didn't wear a hat and his hair was dark, cut short, and crinkly. She thought his eyes were either blue or grey but wouldn't swear to which. His nose, she remembered, had a slightly bashed appearance as if he'd once been a boxer. He was cleanshaven and she guessed his age to be somewhere in the late thirties. She had not paid much attention to his car but she seemed to remember it was big and silver.

Realising there was little more he would be able to learn here Parkinson laid his cup and saucer on the small coffee table and rose slowly to his feet.

Immediately the little woman was all bustle again and escorting him to the door. Parkinson turned as he stepped out on the garden path and held out his big hand. Her small one rested there for a moment like a frightened mouse.

'Thank you for the tea, Mrs Williamson,' he grinned, 'and don't you fret. Your husband will be home soon and you can start thinking about roses.'

Her small, plump figure remained standing forlornly on the doorstep as his big Jaguar pulled away from the kerb and, in a moment, turned the corner and was gone.

Parkinson telephoned Griff from the first non-vandalised telephone box he came to.

'We can strike number one, sir. He hasn't been in the country for three months.'

They had finally decided that Parkinson should investigate

the top six people thrown up on the computer lists before digging deeper into the also-rans, believing that if they were to find a connection with HAWL it would most likely be among those six. Sir Thomas took the news philosophically.

'Oh well, I suppose it was a bit much to expect you'd be lucky on the first try. But at least it means we've eliminated one, four, and six. That leaves you two, three, and five to have a go at.'

'Number six, sir? I didn't know we'd eliminated him?'

Griff coughed slightly.

'We've only just got the news ourselves, Gerald. Poor fellow's gone completely gaga apparently. He's been confined in a mental institution for the past seven weeks. Been kept very quiet, of course. Apparently he still talks to his son as if he were alive. Dreadful thing to happen to a man like that. Absolutely dreadful.'

Resolutely blotting out the thought of one of Britain's greatest athletes going mad Parkinson got back to business.

'Seems as if I've crossed someone else's trail on Williamson, sir.'

Sir Thomas's voice was suddenly sharp. 'Any idea who?'

'No, sir. All Mrs Williamson could tell me was that he had a very slight foreign accent. She'd no idea what kind of accent, of course.'

Griff was silent for a moment. Parkinson listened to the humming on the wire and imagined it was his boss's brain moving into high gear. Presently Sir Thomas spoke again.

'Looks like someone is taking the same approach we are. Trouble is, they may not have arrived at the same list of candidates. Williamson might just have been a lucky shot. We can't second-guess where they might go next. You carry on with your list and I'll see about drafting some extra help. Looks like we are running out of time fast.'

Chapter Nine

James Alistair Fraser, once known to his comrades as 'Big Jaf', was a drinking man. He enjoyed his pint and a few drams at his Sedgefield local and did not appear to mind the sharp vowels of the County Durham locals he drank them with. He was not in favour of the many working men's clubs crowding the county because he preferred that his drinking not be interrupted by bingo callers, twanging guitars, or importuning committee members trying to sell him raffle tickets. In many ways a retiring sort of man 'Big Jaf' much preferred the pub atmosphere. You did not need to become involved unless you particularly wanted to be and you could take all the time you needed to become acquainted with the regulars.

The regulars at the Raven had long been familiar with the big, suntanned, dour faced man who invariably positioned himself at the far corner of the bar and they were equally familiar with his regular absences. The Raven clientele were not particularly curious people and, though most of them had, on some occasion, spent a few sociable hours with the big Scot, it had never occurred to them to enquire as to what the man did for a living. Nor had Fraser volunteered the information. It was generally assumed by the more knowledgeable among them he worked abroad, probably in Africa or Saudi Arabia or some other such place. Occasionally in the course of casual conversation, this assumption was borne out by his casual but familiar reference to some foreign city or other.

These days of course, since his wife had been killed in the Granada Bomb thing all those months ago, the big man had become even more taciturn and morose. But they understood this and respected his obvious desire to be left alone. If he chose to speak, then they were happy to chat with him, if he didn't then they contented themselves with a quick 'hello' or a friendly nod.

His daughter, Moira, was a completely different kettle of fish however. When she was with the big man (and she appeared to spend a great deal more time with him now since her mother's death), the entire bar seemed to light up with the force of her happy extrovert personality.

The regulars loved Moira Fraser. She knew them all by name and, regardless of how busy the bar might be she always took a little time to have a chat. She practically never missed a 'best of three' game of dominoes with old Tommy Currie and his cronies. Tommy, who knew every domino in the pack like a personal friend, somehow always managed to lose to the laughing girl before he would go on to roundly trounce anyone else who dared challenge him. The old domino player would swear on a stack of Bibles it was Moira's gleaming mass of honey-blonde hair which so bedazzled him that he couldn't think straight. Which, coming from an eighty-two year old veteran, was a remarkable compliment to the girl's good looks.

The difference in Jaf when his daughter was present was quite considerable. The sombre, deeply ridged lines of his hard, brown face would relax and soften and his grey eyes would positively beam with pride and pleasure. On such occasions he would laugh and smile a lot. Once or twice, he had even been known to crack a ponderous joke or two. There was no doubt in anyone's mind that Moira was the apple of her father's eye or, for that matter, that the small, slim girl worshipped her father.

There was also no doubt in the regulars' collective minds that where his daughter was concerned Jaf was a very dangerous man indeed.

This realisation had come to them well over a year ago when the quiet man, his wife and his daughter called in for a drink on their way home from some outing. The bar had been much more crowded than normal, the regulars having been augmented by a pack of young football supporters who had been attending a local game. The majority of the football fans were brash, noisy, and, by the time the Frasers arrived, well on the way to making a nuisance of themselves.

Moira and her mother (herself an exceptionally pretty woman with the same vivacious personality as her daughter), attracted immediate attention from the rowdy bunch. Both mother and daughter treated the whistling and clucking with their usual good humour and mixed with the regulars as they always did. Moira, as usual, was immediately challenged to her 'best of three' duel by old man Currie and, knowing she would be allowed to win anyway, happily took her place opposite the old man. Her mother, sensing perhaps that there might be a little trouble, hovered close by the table rather than joining Jaf at his normal spot at the bar.

Several of the rowdies, seeing the two women apparently isolated with a group of harmless, beaming old men who, although they already knew the result of the 'needle match', were cheering on their champion, moved in. At some stage during the game two of the rowdies crowded out Mrs Fraser and one of the remainder made the mistake of trying to goose Moira through the open back of her chair.

As one of the regulars later said, 'Nobody really knew what was happening until bodies started flying over tables and glasses were crashing to the floor all over the place. There was no warning. No shouts of anger. Nothing! One moment Fraser was at the bar with his pint and the next he was among them. Nobody could really believe it was happening. It was like something you'd expect to see in the movies only it wasn't make-believe. It was real.'

The fracas was over as quickly as it began. But, short though it was, one man suffered a broken jaw, another a fractured arm, and two were stretched unconscious. The affair in fact began and ended so quickly that Fraser, his women gathered protectively close, was offering to pay for the damage done before the landlord had time to get round from behind the bar.

The regulars supported Fraser to a man. No action was ever taken by either the landlord or the police. The clientele of the Raven, however, had learned a lesson they would never forget.

Tonight, however, the big Scot was on his own. Moira had

cheerfully declined to accompany him, saying she had far too much to do in the house and besides, it looked as if it might rain. So far it had not rained but there was a raw, biting dampness in the air. Jaf, who invariably walked the mile from his cottage to the Raven, was pleased to leave the chilling darkness for the cheerful familiarity of the bar.

Ordering himself a pint of Exhibition and a quick scotch to chase the chill from his bones, Fraser took up his usual position at the far end of the bar and surveyed the room casually. The place was far from busy. Old Tommy and his cronies had the dominoes clacking cheerfully, two or three of the younger set were playing darts, but aside from two earnest-looking characters arguing with the good natured barman over the respective merits of Sunderland and Newcastle football clubs, he had the bar more or less to himself.

This suited Jaf pretty well.

He did not particularly feel like socialising because he had other things on his mind. The big man was worried about his daughter. In his view Moira was spending far too much of her time with him. He considered that at twenty-two she should be out enjoying herself with young people of her own age instead of trying to take her mother's place. Hell, she shouldn't have to look after that barn of a house the way she did, and she shouldn't spend so much of her time worrying about him. Her attitude to his work was worse than Margaret's had been. Kept telling him he was getting too old for soldiering and he was only forty-six.

Well, maybe in that respect she was right. He had more or less quit now anyway. He had enough cash tucked away to look after them - providing, of course, they didn't go berserk. That was one good thing about being a merc - it paid well and all tax free. Providing you didn't get your head blown off, a few years could set you up quite nicely and probably he'd had a few years too many. The odds were getting shorter.

Now, of course he'd got this other thing to attend to and that should keep him pretty busy for a while. So maybe he just would stay at home. Perhaps then Moira would relax a little, start bringing friends home, make a life for herself. She wouldn't have much to look forward to if he went away again, save perhaps a telegram saying he wouldn't be coming any more.

Fraser invariably took his position at the far end of the bar not because he particularly liked it but because his back was safe and he could keep a watchful eye on the door. It was a habit he had slipped into over the years and one which had stood him in good stead in several odd corners of the world. He was therefore immediately aware of the advent of a tall, brown-haired young man shouldering his way through the swing door.

The big Scot came instantly alert.

The expression on Jaf's face did not alter in the slightest. His eyes betrayed nothing beyond a mild curiosity but the whipcord muscles of the big body now held the relaxed readiness of a hunting cat ready to move on the instant. He had recognised the young man immediately. Not the man himself, of course, but the type. Fraser had run across them before in various countries. Young, tough, finely honed athletic people with the same cautious, wary look in their eyes. The eyes of hunters.

The mercenary watched the young man glance swiftly around the room. Saw the alert, wary eyes flicker over him and knew himself to be recognised for what he was. The stranger leaned across the bar and spoke quietly to the barman. The barman smiled and nodded down the bar towards Jaf before returning to his argument with the two serious students of North Eastern soccer. The tall young man walked directly toward the waiting Scot.

Empty-faced, Fraser watched him approach. He noted the easy, athletic stride, the smartly creased cavalry twill slacks, the well-cut but very, very slightly off balance corduroy jacket. The man was armed. Not an unusual circumstance in Jaf's profession but not what one would expect in a Sedgefield pub.

The young man gave the Scot a friendly grin and held out his hand. There was no smile in the green eyes.

'My name's Parkinson, Mr Fraser. I'd like a few words with you if I may.'

Jaf took the proffered hand but not quite in the conventional manner. Thinking that some of these younger fellows still had a lot to learn he had the fingers folded inwards and his huge paw crushing them tightly before Parkinson could react. Their hands being well below the level of the bar the action went completely unobserved. Parkinson's breath hissed sharply through his teeth at the pain of the vice-like grip. He strove to keep his face from contorting. He had not expected such a reaction in a public place. The huge man had just more or less immobilised him. Even if his hand were to be released immediately there was no way he could go for the Colt Special under his left arm until the feeling came back to his fingers. He was not stupid enough to think he could take Fraser in any other way. The man could probably kill him where he stood.

Jaf smiled pleasantly but there was neither pleasure nor humour in the flat grey eyes.

'Why do you come to see me wearing a gun, Parkinson?'

The pain in his hand was excruciating. Gerald had to fight to keep himself from rising to his toes in reaction.

'Because I'm not the only one looking for you and you may be in danger.'

The pressure on the top joints of his fingers increased.

'Explain!'

As swiftly as he could Parkinson told him of his search for a connection with HAWL. It was, in his opinion, pointless to lie to this man. He was the type who would recognise the truth instantly or keep after it until he finally got it. Jaf heard him through. The pressure on Parkinson's crushed fingers relaxed slightly then his hand was released. The big man grinned sardonically as the younger man thankfully rubbed and flexed his nerveless fingers.

'And do you honestly think that if I'm connected with HAWL I'm going to tell you?'

'No, I don't,' retorted Parkinson. 'But at least I can ask you where you've been this past couple of weeks, and it will be a damned sight quicker checked if *you* tell us. We'll find out in the end anyway.'

Jaf drained his pint and calmly signalled the barman for a refill. The incongruity of the situation struck him and his lips twitched slightly. Christ, if the people in the bar only knew what was going on under their very noses, they'd have all kinds of fits.

'What makes you think someone else may be looking for me?'

Parkinson, some of the feeling back in his fingers, saw no harm in telling the big man. Regardless of whether he was part of HAWL or not he was entitled to know someone could be gunning for him. Briefly he related his discovery on his visit to the Williamson home earlier that day. The Scot's heavy eyebrows lifted.

'Would that be Ken Williamson you're talking about?'

'Yes. D'you know him?'

Jaf grinned.

'Oh aye, I know Ken all right. He's a good man. We've worked on a few jobs together. Twice we've been on the same side. I thought he'd retired, though.'

Parkinson, who, until this moment, had not realised that the circumstances of a mercenary's life could lead them to doing their best to outwit and kill former comrades, felt a cold shudder trickle down his spine. These really were men who fought not only for money but for the sheer pleasure of fighting. They appeared to live in a kill-or-be-killed situation where loyalty was given only to the man who held the purse strings. He wondered if the big man beside him would have felt some kind of remorse had he been forced to kill Williamson in some jungle fire fight. Somehow he doubted it. These were a breed of men apart. They knew the risks and accepted them. In all probability financial reward was a secondary consideration.

'He's in South Africa at the moment,' Parkinson said. 'His wife tells me this is his last job.'

The big Scot nodded and lifted his pint. With the glass halfway to his mouth something occurred to him. His eyes were suddenly once more cold and flat.

'How'd you know I was here, Parkinson? If you've been frightening Moira I'll . . . ' His voice trailed away at the bewildered expression on Parkinson's face. Suddenly there was a snapping savagery in his tone. 'Quick man, did you go to the house?'

'Yes. Yes, I did. The lights were on but there was no reply to my knock. I simply came here on the off chance somebody might know where I could find you.'

The big man's face was like stone.

'How long ago? How long since you were at the house?'

Some of the mercenary's urgency communicated itself to the younger man.

'Not long. Maybe half an hour ago.'

The Scot was already moving. Not quite certain what was happening, but impelled by a sudden sense of foreboding, Gerald Parkinson found himself running after the big man.

Chapter Ten

At precisely the same moment Fraser and Parkinson fled from the Raven, John Lindsay Hughes tossed the book he had been attempting to read agitatedly to one side and uncoiling his spare frame from the comfort of his armchair, began to pace restlessly around his book-lined study. He had not felt truly comfortable with himself since his visit to Sir Thomas Griff. The two more recent killings in Ireland had done little to ease his state of mind.

He had missed something.

With the total conviction of a man charged with the task of drumming facts into frequently unreceptive minds Hughes knew beyond all shadow of a doubt there had been something he had omitted to tell Griff. Whether that something was important or not he had no idea. He had a vague, uncertain feeling that it might be hence his state of considerable agitation. But, regardless of its import, at the moment it was purely academic because he had literally no idea what was troubling him. Something kept niggling at the back of his mind but regardless of how hard he tried it stubbornly refused to come to the surface.

A man to whom violence in any form was a total stranger, Hughes could not really grasp the savagery behind the HAWL killings. Nor, for that matter, could he really understand terrorism or its aims. The very thought of killing in order to instil fear and thus establish a political point was absolute anathema to him. The recent killing of an Indian by Kashmiris residing in England was completely beyond him, as was the statement by an elderly Kashmiri that the young people were becoming angry. If they were so damned angry why pick on their host country in which to perpetrate their murder? Why not take their grievance where it belonged? Although he could not comprehend killing, the linguist knew that the trend somehow had to be stopped. The rule of the law had to be upheld in any society or descent into anarchy would inevitably result.

Thus, as a law-abiding citizen who abhorred violence in any form, it worried him he might be in possession of some tiny piece of information which might possibly help the forces of law and order. But as he wandered restlessly round the big, familiar, comfortable room he could not dredge up from the back of his mind that tiny piece of information his subconscious kept warning him he had overlooked.

He knew he was going to spend another restless, dream-haunted night.

Chapter Eleven

Moira Fraser watched her father shrug into his battered sheepskin jacket and smiled quietly to herself. Jaf enjoyed his pint at the Raven and most nights he would take a walk down and have one or two. She knew, although the big man would never admit it, that he enjoyed the company and was beginning to think of himself as one of the regulars.

This suited Moira fine. Although she knew her father enjoyed a drink she had never, in her life, seen him drunk and she took his nightly trips as a sign that he was beginning to become more settled in his mind and that his soldiering days were really over. He'd been home for nearly three months now which was as long as she could ever remember him staying at one stretch. If only her mother could have seen this happening.

Moira was well aware of how hard her father had been hit by her mother's death. While understanding it and sympathising with him, it had come as quite a shock to her that a man so strong and self-contained could crumple so swiftly when someone they love has been taken from them suddenly. By the time they had got him out of Angola and home her mother had been in her grave six days. Moira did not think she would ever be fully rid of the memory of his face as they had stood together by her mother's last resting place. Nor would she forget the great, strangled, wrenching sobs jolting his massive frame or the gentle loving way he had patted the raw earth with his huge hand. It had almost been as if he had been caressing her mother's face as she had seen him do a thousand times in his dour, inarticulate way when she had been alive.

Something had happened to the big man in those few minutes they had spent by the grave. Moira did not know what had taken place but she knew instinctively something had changed inside him. She had, like a woman, put it down to the terrible sense of loss he must have felt.

Moira had tried, in the few days he was at home, to give him as much love and comfort as was in her power. But for most of those days he had sat, stonefaced, in the living room, gazing blankly across the hearth to the empty chair where her mother had normally sat. He had never gone back to the grave. Ten days after he had come home he had gone off again to fight someone else's dirty war.

Now he had been home almost three months and was showing little sign of ever wanting to leave again. Quite the opposite in fact. There was nothing of the old feeling of transience which had always been with him before, and, though Moira had always been aware of his love he had taken to showing it in a hundred different ways. Almost as if he wanted to be certain she would never have any doubts about his feeling for her.

Moira, in her turn, because she had always cherished the big dour man, responded like a nurtured flower. In spite of his protests she had thrown up her job with a Newcastle advertising agency and now devoted her time to looking after her big, lost father. She would, she told him repeatedly, return to the agency when she was certain he was settled and happy.

And so they had gone on.

Of late, however, there had been a new restlessness in the big man and it had begun to worry her. Two or three times recently he had been gone for a day or two on what he called business trips. On each occasion he had appeared even more restless when he returned. When taxed by his daughter he had been oddly reticent about his trips and she'd had to be content with his reply that she would find out 'all in good time'.

The big man opened the front door on his way out.

'Don't be late, Dad,' she called.

'I won't, pet,' he replied and was gone into the dark November night.

Moira Fraser was never to be certain how long her father had been gone before the heavy brass knocker clattered loudly against the front door.

She was in the kitchen preparing the pastry for her father's favourite apple tart when the sharp rattle echoed through the house. Consequently she was still wiping floury hands when she opened the door to face a smiling, round faced young man wearing gold rimmed spectacles. Moira had a brief glimpse of the headlights of a large car pulling away from the gate before, in a sudden blur of movement, something struck her a vicious blow across her left temple.

The smiling young man vanished in a vivid flash of light. She had a quick sensation of sickness then her knees hit the polished tiles of the hall floor. She realised vaguely she had fallen as another jarring blow rocked her head sideways on the slim column of her neck. She was not aware of the third or fourth blows as they smashed her into complete oblivion.

As Parkinson's Jaguar hurtled away from the Raven and raced along unfamiliar, narrow, hedge-lined roads, the younger man concentrated totally on his driving and put all thought from his mind of the big, strangely still man crushed into the bucket seat beside him. Something, he knew, was desperately wrong, but this was not the time to ask questions. As the headlights picked out an isolated row of six or seven houses, Jaf spoke harshly: 'Pull in by those houses.'

Parkinson did not argue. He was aware that Fraser's house lay a few hundred yards away around the twisting bends of the narrow road but guessed the big man must have a good reason for his barked command. Besides, in the two or three minutes he had been driving, he had become decidedly claustrophobic. Being in a confined space with Fraser was like being caged with a tiger. Jaf had the door open before the car pulled to a stop. He positively flowed out of the car and Parkinson was again forcibly reminded of a huge predatory animal.

'Right, Parkinson. Put the lights out and come out. Look quick about it.'

Parkinson, thankful for the heavy drag of the Colt under his arm, did as he was bid. The big, sheep skinned Scot, looming over Parkinson's six foot by at least five inches, draped a massive arm around his shoulders. Gerald all but flinched.

'Now, laddie,' hissed Fraser. 'We're going to walk from here and you're going to be pissed. Understand me? Pissed as a bloody rat.'

Not waiting for Parkinson to reply, Jaf, the young man pinned firmly beside him, set off staggering down the dark roadway bellowing 'Blaydon Races' like a wounded buffalo. Far from being slow on the uptake Parkinson immediately joined in. The big man was obviously fearful something had happened at his cottage. To get to the cottage a stranger would require a car. And, if a trap was being set for the big man, the car had to be hidden close by or Jaf would be alerted by its presence at the gate. Therefore they were pretending to be drunk to put a possible look-out off guard, and they were looking for a vehicle parked off the road somewhere – probably in a gateway to a field.

As they staggered drunkenly down the centre of the road, Parkinson's eyes began to adjust to the night and he was able to pick out the stark outlines of the hedgerows readily enough. He became aware of the deeper, more solid shadow of the big Rover in the same instant as Fraser's arm tightened warningly on his shoulder. The pair tottered on, making the night hideous with a raucous rendering of 'Annie Laurie' until they drew abreast of the parked vehicle. The red glow of a cigarette gleamed for a moment in the dark interior.

Fraser stopped abruptly. Swaying like a great tree in a high wind he peered exaggeratedly toward the car.

'Hey, Geordie,' he slurred. 'We've a courtin' couple here.' He cackled drunkenly. 'What d'ye bet it's wee Mary Sloane again. Dif – dif – dif – new boy-friend for every night in the week, yon lass. We'll ha' a wee look hinny.'

Parkinson teetering behind him, the big man swayed towards the car. Stooping, he peered owlishly through the window. The man jammed behind the wheel obviously did not like being studied like a goldfish in a bowl. With the obvious intention of giving a pair of drunken country cousins a tongue lashing he wound down the window.

It was a mistake.

As the window came down a massive arm shot into the car with the speed of a striking Mamba to curl around the startled man's head and drag him head first into the air. As the man's head came through the open window Parkinson suddenly realised what was about to happen and moved to cover the two paces between him and Fraser. Even as he did so his mind was signalling he was too late. Jaf suddenly threw his weight towards the rear of the car smashing the exposed neck against the back section of the window frame. With a sound like the breaking of a damp stick the man died without uttering a sound.

Parkinson, himself no stranger to death or killing, felt the blood drain from his face at the casual ease with which Jaf had just taken a life. He watched the big man contemptuously push the corpse back into the seat and reach into the vehicle to produce an ugly M52 automatic pistol from the shelf below the dash. Expertly he removed the magazine, checked the load, then slipped it back into the butt.

'Bastard wasn't taking any chances. Had this under his hand when he wound the window down. Now let's get out of here. God knows what's happening at the cottage.'

They covered the short distance between the parked car and Fraser's cottage at a fast run. The house, once a farm worker's two-room-and-kitchen home, had been extended considerably over the years and was now a long, low, single storey structure which might have been classified as 'ranch style'. The lights appeared to have been left on in every room. Crouching behind a four-foot privet hedge which guarded the front gardens they paused a moment to take stock of the situation. Parkinson noted with something like awe that Fraser was not even breathing heavily. The big man had even found time and wind to explain that he had left his daughter alone in the house. This, however, did not, in Parkinson's mind, give the Scot the right to kill a man virtually on sight. He muttered as much to Fraser as they peered through the hedge.

'Don't talk like a bloody idiot, Parkinson,' the big man hissed angrily. 'And don't take me for a fool. Your orders are to find out if I'm a part of HAWL, get as much info out of me as you can and then quietly see me off. Since those other bastards obviously don't work for you I take it that they are on the same errand except they will not be asking questions. Now you can cut the holier-than-thou shit' – Parkinson heard the soft snick as the safety came off the automatic – 'and make up your mind whether you're with me or not because I'm going to see what I'm up against and killing you won't make a great deal of difference to me.'

Parkinson nodded. 'All right, you bastard. But sooner or later you and I are going to settle up.'

The Scot sniffed. 'Stay here. I'm going to have a look around.'

Jaf vanished abruptly into the darkness leaving Parkinson feeling as if he had been talking to a ghost. He strained his eyes towards the lighted windows of the house. Once he thought he caught a glimpse of a flickering shadow but could not be sure. Easing the snub-nosed Colt Special from its holster he cocked it with a practised movement of his thumb. Gerald far preferred the cylinder action Colt to the automatics. When the chips were down there was considerably less danger of jamming. That, in his opinion, was worth considerably more than maybe, just maybe, getting off one more shot than the other fellow.

He thought about Fraser. If ever there was a candidate for HAWL Jaf had to be it. A highly trained, superbly fit fighting machine with the acknowledged, if not quite legal, rank of Major among his colleagues. How hard must that rank have been won? It indicated brains, leadership, courage and a certain cold-blooded calculating attitude towards death. Fraser's activities over the past fourteen days or so would certainly bear some examination but, if he did appear connected with HAWL, then taking him, either dead or alive, would prove no easy matter.

Fraser's big hand fell lightly on his shoulder. Parkinson had neither seen nor heard his approach. The big man hunkered beside him.

'One of the windows I can't see through. The drapes are drawn too tight. But I could only see one man in the entire house and there's nobody around the outside. The man inside is a husky-looking young fellow wearing glasses. He's waiting in the living room with what looks like a Walther P38 in his hand. We're not going to have too much of a chance surprising the bastard because from where he's standing he can cover both the door *and* the window. The only thing we've really got in our favour is that he'll only be expecting one man to come through the door.'

The big man paused and for a second Parkinson caught the glitter of his white teeth as he bared them in a mirthless grin.

'Now, if two of us go at him simultaneously but from different angles it might be another matter. We don't, of course, know how fast he will be with that gun. Not quite fast enough, I would think, to drop us both. There's no sign of Moira so I'm guessing she will be in the study . . . that's the window to the right of the door, the living room is on the left. Here's what we're going to do.'

Christ, Parkinson thought, he's giving me orders as if I were one of his troops. Nevertheless he held his tongue and listened attentively.

'*You* are going to go through the front door. Or at least he's going to think you're coming through the door because you are going to kick it open with as much bloody noise as possible. While you're doing that I'm going to get him through the window. Have you got that?'

Parkinson, adrenalin beginning to course through his veins, nodded in the darkness.

'What happens if you don't get him?'

Fraser grunted. 'Laddie, whoever these people are they're professionals. If I don't get him then you won't have to worry about whether I'm part of HAWL or not because I simply will not be around to answer any more of your stupid questions. Now, let's go!'

John Laverock Houston liked the weighty heft of the P38 in his hand. The two-pound drag on his wrist gave him a sense of power, raised him far above the level of ordinary men and imbued him with an almost God-like superiority. With the Walther in his hand he held the power of life and death over other mortals and this gave him enormous satisfaction. Because J.L. Houston was a born killer.

Houston was one of the few who had actually enjoyed Viet Nam. It was there he had first learned the deadly power of the gun; saw how men could cower before its imperious snout; savoured the white hot pleasure of taking another human life. It was here that he came to the attention of other, more remote men to whom lives were mere weights, balancing the razor edge of the scales of World Power.

J.L.H. left the army with a sense of keen regret. Wearing the uniform of his country he had been able to kill with impunity because his country told him it was his duty to do so. He was recruited almost immediately to play the same role as a civilian and again he was told it was his duty.

In just over five years Houston had removed eleven men and two women from the land of the living. He had asked no questions and had never been given explanations. Perhaps the people he had killed had been enemies of the state. Communist agents, perhaps, or traitors in highly dangerous positions. He never knew why the people he killed had been marked for death because he did not need to know. All he required was the identity of the target, and the pleasure of the kill outweighed all else.

Not, of course, that Houston was not well paid.

Regularly as clockwork he was in receipt of a handsome monthly retainer paid in cash and, upon successful completion of each sanction, a very handsome five figure bonus would be deposited into his Swiss bank account. It did not trouble him that the money could never be traced back to its origin or that he had never been absolutely certain as to who his employer was. For him it was enough that possible police intervention was successfully side-tracked and that he was very happy at his work.

Houston, beyond what he had read in the press, was completely ignorant of HAWL. He and Lawson (now on watch somewhere along the road) had been flown from Germany and Belgium respectively in US military aircraft and given two targets. This man Fraser was the first of them. They had three days in which to carry out the two sanctions, then they would be flown out again. The stupid Brits would never even know they had been in the country.

He thought about the girl he had clobbered. It was a real pity about her because she was a pretty little fox. Still, she had seen him and that was enough. She'd still been alive when he had dragged her into the study, so he'd have to make certain she was dead before he left. Not that her being able to identify him would make much difference, but he liked to keep his trail fairly clean.

Something crashed heavily against the front door forcing it violently open and smashing it back on its hinges against the inside wall. Houston dropped into a half crouch at the first crashing thud and snapped up the Walther to level it at the open door between the living room and the hall. In the same instant as the heavy door smashed against the inside wall the entire wood-framed window imploded and a huge figure hurtled into the room. As his head swivelled sharply at this new intrusion the last things John Laverock Houston saw were the window drapes still billowing inwards, shards of glass cascading in all directions, and the ugly black muzzle of the M52.

The first of the high powered 7.62 bullets travelling at a velocity of 1600 feet per second took half of Houston's head away and sent his spectacles falling in a glittering arc towards the floor. As the impact of the first lifted him spinning off his feet, the second and third shots smashed into his chest, tore straight through him, and buried themselves beyond recovery in the far end of the room.

Chapter Twelve

'You appear to have stirred up quite a hornet's nest, Gerald,' said Sir Thomas Griff through his usual cloud of cigar smoke. 'Durham Constabulary have been creating all kinds of hell. Very blunt people up there, you know. Seems they don't like their countryside being littered with strange corpses. I've had to roust the Home Secretary in order to calm them down a little and he, poor man, is not exactly pleased about it either because I understand he spoke to the PM and he is positively frothing.' He peered up through the smoke at the tired, drawn face of Gerald Parkinson and added, a little more kindly, 'Sit down, Gerald for heaven's sake. You look about all in.'

The little man waited until his agent had settled himself comfortably, then leaned across his paper free desk.

'Now, ignoring the fact you've been giving Durham Police all kinds of fits, suppose you tell me from the beginning everything that happened up there.'

Parkinson, who had managed less than an hour's sleep in the past thirty-six and who had just flown down from Teeside after having been summoned peremptorily to base, took a moment or two to marshal his thoughts. The piercing blue eyes of his chief focussed unblinkingly on his tired face. Griff heard him through in absolute silence not even thanking one of his pretty secretaries as she entered quietly with two steaming cups of strong coffee. Presently the little man stirred and ran his fingers through his shock of tousled grey hair.

'What do you think, Gerald? CIA?'

Parkinson nodded tiredly. 'Yes, sir. I think so. Not regular

Company men, of course, but I would definitely put them down as a pair from 'S' section. There's no doubt they were American.'

Griff sucked at his cigar thoughtfully. The 'S', or Sanction Section, of the Central Intelligence Agency had been in existence for a considerable number of years. Nobody really knew for certain who controlled it or how much of the Company's concealed financial appropriations were funnelled into it but its brief was fairly widely recognised among Intelligence people. 'S' personnel were, in fact, a nameless, faceless group of killers whose job it was to remove people from the path of progress - *CIA* progress. As various Presidents had worked hard at pulling the teeth of the Company, so had 'S' section gone deeper and deeper underground. Of late, however, with the new upsurge of national pride under the current administration a number of peculiar deaths had led to the inevitable conclusion that 'S' Section was not only alive and well but was coming in out of the cold. If Parkinson was right, and Sir Thomas did not for one moment dispute this, then the Americans were taking HAWL very seriously indeed.

Griff blew a stream of smoke towards the ceiling then took a sip at his scalding coffee.

If the Americans took HAWL seriously enough to go on the warpath then it was a thousand to one that the Russians were going to do exactly the same thing and that was not a particularly pleasant thought. The Superpowers had long ago discovered it was an expensive business killing off each other's agents on a tit-for-tat basis and sanctions were now only resorted to in cases of extreme necessity - occasionally with each other's connivance. The HAWL business could readily swing them back at each other's throats. Not that Griff objected to them killing each other off but the thought that some of his own people might be caught in the middle was something else. Good people were too damned hard to come by these days. The other British Intelligence Agencies were one thing, but his bunch were rather special and not to be squandered profligately. He turned his mind back to the immediate problem.

'Tell me,' he said quietly. 'What do you think of this man Fraser?'

Gerald cleared his throat.

'Well, sir, he's a very dangerous man and he definitely could be one of the people we're looking for. He is, without doubt, one of the most ruthless men I have ever met.'

'You say "could be", Gerald. I take it you're not sure he is one of our men?'

'Things were pretty hairy up there, sir. To be honest I never got around to questioning him in any detail. But in all fairness I have to say that if anyone could be capable of HAWL type killings, it *has* to be him.'

'What do you suggest then, Gerald?' The melodious voice might have been talking to the local vicar about the next garden fete. 'Do you think we should, like our American friends, make arrangements for his – er – removal on a "just-in-case" basis, or wait to see what might come out in the wash?'

Parkinson knew damned well his chief had already made his decision regarding Fraser and was simply using him as a sounding board. Nevertheless he thought for a moment or two before giving his answer.

'No, sir. I don't think we should do that. Better we should keep a very close eye on Fraser for a time before we do anything. If he is part of HAWL then there is always the possibility he might lead us to the rest of the bunch and the wait would be worth it. Candidly, if HAWL are as determined as they appear to be I doubt if the removal of one man – even one as dangerous as Fraser – is going to stop them. We *have* to get to the head, and Fraser could be our only lead.'

'What if Fraser is the leader of the group?' Griff asked quietly.

'I thought of that too, sir. But even if he is the brains behind this it's still going to take a certain amount of time to prove it. I mean we just can't remove him on the off-chance.'

Griff nodded thoughtfully.

'So what you're telling me is that we should allow a highly dangerous man to run around loose until we find out a little more about him. What happens if he makes a run for it and gets out of the country? What do we do then?'

Parkinson smiled grimly.

'As it happens, sir, Fraser has an Achilles heel. He is extraordinarily fond of his daughter and there is simply no way he would place her in a position where she could be harassed, hurt, possibly killed. If we have the daughter we can control Fraser.'

Griff, his cigar temporarily in the ashtray, steepled his fingers.

'Yes, I think you have the rights of it, Gerald. We'll go your way – for a time anyway. How is the girl, by the way?'

Gerald Parkinson raised his hand in an oddly benedictory gesture.

'Pretty badly beaten about the head, sir. Right now she's in Darlington General Hospital. She was still unconscious when I left, but the quacks seem to think she's going to be all right. I've – ah – I've arranged a round the clock guard on her, sir, but told them to keep it discreet. We don't want the hospital overrun with large men in blue uniforms and heavy boots.'

Sir Thomas looked at his agent thoughtfully.

'So you think someone else might realise the girl is the key to the father. Is that it?'

'Yes, sir. It struck me she would be pretty vulnerable in a public hospital so I – er – I took your name in vain a little and prevailed on the local bobbies.'

A smile flickered on the little man's face for a moment. He carefully retrieved his cigar from the overflowing ashtray and puffed at it tentatively for a moment.

'Right, Gerald. I'm more or less in the picture now. I think you should get yourself off and pick up a few hours sleep before you head North again. It seems you might need a little help so I'll put someone else to checking out the other pair on your list. You stick with Fraser, he seems to be our best bet so far.'

As Parkinson hoisted his muscular frame from his chair Griff smiled again. 'In the meantime,' he said. 'I think I'll have a word with our American friends.'

Charles Hamilton, in spite of his ancestry, did not particularly like the British. He thought them effete, slightly decadent, definitely eccentric, undoubtedly lazy, living on past glories, and a general pain in the ass. He disliked what he considered their superior attitude, hated their undisputable history and cordially disliked their disgusting habit of drinking warm beer. But most of all he disliked himself because, despite their innumerable faults, he found himself still slightly in awe of the people who had created the greatest Empire the world had ever known. Accordingly he arrived to lunch with Sir Thomas Griff bearing an Everest-sized chip on his shoulder. At first he had been tempted to refuse the telephone invitation but caution and curiosity had prevailed. He had been well warned of this man before he had taken up his position as London Head of Station. Although they had not yet met, he was aware that Sir Thomas Griff was not a man to be trifled with.

On his arrival at Griff's club he was delighted when an ancient waiter ushered him to his host's table and he discovered the knight was little more than a goddamned midget. He promptly made the most of his seventy-four inch height by standing as close as possible to the small man while they shook hands, thus forcing Sir Thomas to either tilt his head back or greet his immaculate shirt front. If the diminutive knight noticed the deliberate insult he made no comment and was courteous to a degree.

Through the fairly lengthy meal Griff further infuriated the tall American by maintaining a steady flow of completely inconsequential chatter and making no reference whatsoever to the purpose behind the meeting. This was yet another facet of the British character which irritated the visitor. There appeared to be no way in which you could force them to come to the point until they were good and ready. He tried to strike back by complaining to his host about the slowness of the service offered by the old men creeping about the large dining room.

'You know, Sir Thomas,' he said gratingly as an ancient waiter, having served the grouse, limped away from the table. 'If we were in the States these old guys would have been pensioned off years ago.'

Something flickered momentarily in Griff's blue eyes but he smiled pleasantly enough.

'Ah yes,' he said quietly. 'But that's just it, you see. This is Britain and, in a way, those men *are* pensioners. You see the War took all of the Club's young men. George yonder' – he nodded towards the retreating back of the waiter – ' was one of the very few we ever got back. He – er – he left a leg at Dieppe and he will continue to work here until *he* decides it is time for him to go.'

The American fumed silently and made no further comment. It was over coffee and brandy that Griff fired his first shot.

'I asked you here, Hamilton, to advise you that we have two corpses belonging to you and, with our limited budget, I'd be most grateful if you would take them off our hands. It's very difficult for us to expense funerals you know. A lunch or two, perhaps, but funerals *do* look a bit odd.'

The American gawped like a landed fish. 'Did you say *two* corpses?'

Griff toyed with his brandy glass. 'Yes, I believe that was the figure I quoted. There may be more, of course, but for the moment the – er – body count, as you chaps so delicately put it, is precisely two. They are both from your 'S' Section so I assume you will be quite agreeable to taking this quite unnecessary expense off our hands. Under the circumstances a substantial contribution to Durham Constabulary Widows and Orphans Fund would also not come amiss.'

Sir Thomas stripped the cellophane from a Napoleon and watched the American from under hooded eyes. It gave him some satisfaction to break the news to the CIA man but it was patently obvious Hamilton had been aware of the killers being in the country. He might not have known their target (which was unlikely because the information on Granada Bomb victims *had* to have come through him), but he certainly had known they were there and why.

'Dead, you say?'

The CIA man was trying to bring himself back under control. Griff's bolo punch had jolted him considerably. He was forcing his brain into top gear. Griff smiled thinly.

'Oh yes, they're quite dead old chap. Corpses usually are, you know.'

Seething, Hamilton elected to ignore the little man's gentle sarcasm.

'What happened? How'd they die? Some kind of accident?'

Griff noted there was no disclaimer, no denial of ownership. The arrogant bastard didn't seem to care the killers had been operating illegally in a friendly country. He smiled grimly to himself.

'No. It wasn't exactly an accident, old chap. One had his neck broken - rather efficiently, I believe - and the other had most of his head shot off.'

'Jesus Christ! Do you know who killed them?'

Again the little man showed his thin smile.

'Oh yes. *We* did, I'm afraid.'

The American made a strangled, explosive sound deep in the back of his throat. His lean face suffused a deep red and the veins in his neck stood out like cords. His fists clenched until the knuckles gleamed whitely through the skin and for a moment it looked as if he were about to hurl himself across the table and smash at the little man. Griff watched him impassively. Hamilton got himself under control.

'You - you can sit there and calmly inform me your people have killed two of our men. Two *Americans*!'

Quite suddenly Sir Thomas Griff underwent an extraordinary metamorphosis. The pleasant, well-mannered little person vanished abruptly as if he had never been and the full force of his enormous personality struck the American like a physical blow. Blue eyes gleaming with an almost incandescent light, hook nose poised like the beak of an eagle, Griff leaned forward slightly and appeared, to his astonished guest, to loom over him like a colossus. Charles Hamilton felt distinctly nervous.

'Since when, Hamilton, have Americans gained the mandate to walk on water? Those men were in the country illegally. They were surprised and killed while attempting to take the life of a British citizen. I doubt very much if we will find any record of their arrival in the United Kingdom, therefore it is highly probable they came in with the connivance of the American armed forces who *are* allowed a considerable amount of leeway because we are supposed to be allies.

'Now, we are getting just a little tired of people taking advantage of us and *you*, Hamilton, took advantage. We may not be much by your reckoning but when we become angry we tend to be very angry. Right now, Hamilton, in your own vernacular, I am thoroughly pissed off and am seriously considering asking that you be removed from the country. With very good reason, I may add.'

The CIA man flinched slightly as the smaller man stabbed in his direction with his cigar. He knew perfectly well Griff was making no idle threat. The little man probably had enough on the company to hang him ten times over. All it needed was someone to start an investigation into CIA activities among the NATO countries and the fat would really be in the fire. He cleared his throat, preparatory to saying something, but the little man had not yet finished.

'Hamilton, before you leave this table you can decide that either we co-operate on this HAWL thing or I blow the whistle on you. And that, my friend, includes your calling off any other 'S' Section thugs you may have running loose. Over here we like to launder our own dirty linen and do it as privately as possible.'

Chapter Thirteen

Anne Parkinson, as she prepared herself for bed, was fairly well pleased with herself. In spite of her fears to the contrary, Bill Wilkinson had turned up for their date. He had gone to considerable trouble to make himself look reasonably presentable and, although he still looked as if his clothes were a size too large for him and that he would be better off in hospital, he had succeeded fairly well. He was also almost sober.

Understandably, in spite of the almost deserted intimacy of the little restaurant she had taken him to, he had been shy and self-conscious. Almost painfully so. He had said very little, leaving her to make most of the conversational running. But she had not found this particularly arduous because he was, she discovered, a particularly good listener. Anne had made no attempt to draw him on his feelings over the Granada Bomb incident believing that such an intrusion before he had learned to trust her might send him scuttling back to his shell. There would be time enough for that later when he had become more accustomed to her company and understood what she was trying to do. Meanwhile, since he had displayed no interest in why she should want to be in his company, she thought it more productive to discover a little more about the man himself. It might be useful later as background to her story.

Wilkinson had been almost pathetic in his efforts to please her, hastening, like a boy on his first date, to pass her salt, salad, sauces, whether she required them or not. Although, generally speaking, he had not had a great deal to say for himself, he had managed to eat a little and had struggled to keep his drinking down. She had taken this as a compliment and, to her own amazement, had found herself ridiculously pleased by it.

Anne had found him an educated, articulate, well travelled man, somewhat reticent about himself but forthcoming and complimentary when speaking of others. He appeared, basically, to be the type of person who invariably found something nice to say about others and tried hard to overlook their shortcomings. And yet, with all of that, she sensed somewhere inside him there lay an iron core, possibly a trifle rusted at the moment, but nevertheless, still there somewhere. She found this vaguely disconcerting because it did not tie up with what she knew and was learning of the man.

During the meal, as he picked somewhat listlessly at his food Anne noticed a small tattoo of the Sphinx on his left wrist just about where his watch would have been worn. She asked him about it because he did not appear to be the type of man prone to such decoration.

He grinned rather sheepishly and gently massaged his wrist as if it suddenly pained him.

'I had that done on my first overseas posting in the service. We were all a lot younger then, of course, and quite a lot of us thought it was the manly thing to do. I've kept meaning to have it taken off – or at least I did until – until – ' His voice trailed away and he stared blankly into space for a few moments. Anne's heart suddenly ached for this drawn, desperately sick-looking man. He snapped back to reality suddenly. 'I – I'm sorry, Anne. My mind keeps wandering a little these days. I guess I'm getting old.'

This was the closest he had come to talking about the tragedy but Anne knew it would all come out eventually. Sooner or later the floodgates would open and she would have her story. Strangely the story had somehow become a secondary consideration in her mind and she could not quite understand why.

Wilkinson, miraculously, had not been quite drunk when she drove him back to the disgusting building he lived in. They sat companionably in the car for a moment or two almost as if they were loath to be parted. Anne, suddenly finding the courage she had been lacking all evening, delved into her handbag and produced an envelope which she handed to Wilkinson as he finally clambered out of the car.

'Bill,' and her voice held a sort of desperate urgency combined with what might have been pleading, 'I know you're short of money. This will tide you over for a little while. I – I'll see you on Tuesday.' Then she drove off smartly leaving him standing rather forlornly on the pavement with the envelope clutched in his hand.

He knew they were there. They had been following him all day. They knew he was in this block somewhere but at least they could not possibly know which flat he was in because they would have no idea what name he would be using or even if he actually lived here at all. They could be certain he had come into the building and possibly that he had not left it. Beyond that they did not really know very much except that he was not what he appeared to be, and that, possibly, would be enough to warrant his execution. The question was whether or not they were working their way methodically through a list or simply picking names at random. If they had a list of even only a few names it might help because whoever had turned them loose might not be certain at exactly which point on the list they had begun their search. A small list would undoubtedly narrow the field and shorten the odds but he thought he could live with that for a while.

He wondered briefly who they were and where they had come from, then he decided it did not really matter very much. Whoever they were they were a hindrance and something had to be done about that. Besides, how long would it take them to tie him down to Tony Kaffray? Somehow he did not think it would take too long now that they had him nailed to Bradford Tower.

He sighed and continued soaping his muscular body. Probably even now they would be brandishing a fistful of fivers under somebody's nose in an effort to pin him down to a definite flat. Not that it would do them much good because the man who had come through the entrance bore little resemblance to the man who lived here. But he was a familiar visitor to the Tower and someone may have seen him come to the flat.

It was a pity because he quite liked the place. Unfortunately it was finished for him now.

Showering the soap away he stepped from the shower cubicle and towelled himself vigorously. Hard, powerful muscle rippled and knotted along his arms and shoulders and corrugated on his flat belly. Tony Kaffray was a man in the peak of physical condition. His skin glowed with a sleek, pink lustre as he padded from the bathroom and began to dress humming quietly to himself as he did so. He had made up his mind as to what had to be done. There was little point in waiting.

Presently, immaculate in a dark blue suit and short top coat he emerged from the apartment with a suitcase in each hand. Leaving the suitcases in the thickly carpeted corridor he stepped back inside for a moment. When he reappeared he closed the door very carefully behind him, hefted the suitcases and made his way to the elevator which would carry him down to the underground car park.

Victor Togulev and Vasili Svetanko had been in the United Kingdom for some years. Both were lesser diplomats assigned to the Soviet Embassy. Both, as far as the British Security Services were concerned, had hitherto led completely blameless lives. They had made no attempt whatsoever to break from the rules governing the behaviour of Embassy personnel. They were, it seemed, minor officials bogged down in the quagmire of paper which exists in all such establishments and happy to be working in such a prized posting. They were most certainly not the type to jeopardise their positions by becoming involved in any extra-curricular skullduggery.

Both men were still in their thirties, both were single, both carried out their duties with the minimum of fuss, and both quietly enjoyed those delights of London which fell within their limited means. Both men had pleasant, friendly, extrovert personalities and both were highly trained killers.

Victor was a burly, broad-faced, and, to his disgust, prematurely balding man of around average height. Vasili was the tall, slightly battered looking man whose accent Mrs Williamson had been unable to place. Victor and Vasili, like others in the Embassy, had been placed there years before to be used only in cases of extreme emergency. When the emergency was resolved, probably with a killing, they would be transferred immediately to more friendly nations or simply returned to Mother Russia. Their usefulness in London would then have come to an end.

Neither man was particularly happy to have been winkled from his safe, comfortable job but they knew there was little option. The KGB tended to frown upon those who questioned their orders and neither man was prepared to face such consequences.

The orders had been simple enough. They were furnished with a list of six names and told to dispose of the people listed. Nothing else. No reason given. Not even a preferred method of assassination, no hint it should look like a series of accidents, simply find them, kill them, and move on.

The Russians were not certain what they had uncovered when they had followed their man here because they had no idea why they were supposed to kill him. All they really knew was that this was definitely not the address they had been given and that the target was definitely not what he was supposed to be. They had argued for a time as to whether they should contact the Embassy concerning the target's peculiar behaviour, but had finally decided against it. Their instructions had been quite explicit. Best to get the job done and report afterwards.

They knew, from the neat resident list displayed in the foyer, that their man was not registered there - at least not under his own name. They knew also that he had not reappeared, therefore he was still inside the tall building or had eluded them by simply walking straight through and exiting to the rear somewhere.

Sitting in the front seat of a big Ford they were arguing as to what they should do next when a snappy black Mercedes glided to a halt alongside them. The Mercedes' window slid silently down and the driver, a dark-haired man in his forties, leaned out.

'I say,' he said loudly. 'I say, do you chaps realise you're in my parking spot?'

Victor, sitting nearest the Mercedes, wound down the window of the Ford. Vasili, behind the wheel, leaned forward slightly to see the cause of the interruption.

'What did you say?' Victor asked politely.

'I said,' repeated the Mercedes' driver testily, 'that you chaps are in my parking place. I generally leave my car here for a fast getaway in the mornings.'

Involuntarily Victor turned his head towards his partner as if to confer as to what they should do. Vasili leaned further over the wheel in order to see round the smaller man and get a better view of the Mercedes' driver. His eyes widened suddenly in alarm and his mouth opened to shout a warning.

The warning never came.

A 9mm slug from the silenced Walther P38 he had seen coming over the edge of the open Mercedes window smashed into his skull and the sound was stillborn. Victor, his hand instinctively leaping towards the Tokarev TT33 he carried in a shoulder holster, whipped his head round. The second shot from the Walther tore up through his left eye to exit, in a bloody spray of bone and brain matter, through his bald patch.

The man behind the wheel of the Mercedes calmly tossed the P38 on the cushion of the seat beside him, slipped the car into gear, and cruised unhurriedly away.

Chapter Fourteen

If Sir Thomas Griff could be said to have been bent out of shape by the American intervention in the HAWL affair then he was distorted beyond all recognition when he learned the Soviets had apparently also been caught with their red hands in the cookie jar.

The information came to him via a telephone call from New Scotland Yard at 2.30 a.m. on Saturday, the only day of the week which the little man considered sacrosanct because it was the one day on which he permitted himself an extra hour of sleep and, to his secretary's great joy, never arrived at the office before 7.30. He was, therefore, not in a particularly cheerful frame of mind as he snatched the telephone from its cradle before it had completed its second ring.

'Yes?' he barked.

'This is Chief Superintendent Haws at New Scotland Yard, sir,' said a deferential voice in his ear. 'I've been asked to inform you that at 1.45 this morning we were called to a shooting at Bradford Tower. There are two men dead, sir.'

'Yes, yes,' snapped the little man testily. 'But what has that to do with me? Dammit, don't you realise what time it is?'

'Yes, sir,' the voice said huffily, 'I'm well aware of the time. But the two men who were killed were Russians. *Armed* Russians, sir,' the Chief Super added with a touch of malice.

Griff was aware of a sudden cold chill in the room.

'All right, Chief Superintendent, I apologise for being a trifle waspish. Now would you please take your time and tell me the whole story from the beginning.'

* * *

Colonel Anatoli Leonov was very disturbed.

The violent deaths of Togulev and Svetanko did not particularly perturb him. They had been expendable. They had been well aware of the risks involved in their work and, as far as he was concerned, that was the end of it. But their deaths had created complications which were not going to be so easily overcome.

The Embassy had been called immediately the identity of the pair had been discovered, which had not been particularly difficult as the idiots had been carrying their own driving licences. Been living far too long in this damned country probably. He, in his supposed capacity as personnel administrator, had gone to the scene immediately, taking with him a handful of men and an ambulance.

He had tried to persuade the policeman in charge of the Investigation, a Chief Inspector McLuskey, to release the bodies to him immediately. He had run up against a brick wall and had been most undiplomatically refused. He had then fallen back on the age-old Russian tactic of hectoring bluster and threats of serious International repercussions. The Chief Inspector, a large, florid-faced man with tired, haunted eyes, finally rounded on him exasperatedly.

'Look! I don't know how you do things in Russia, and I don't much bloody care. But *we* have our own way of doing things here and you and your bunch of bully boys are getting in the way of us doing it.' Holding up a hand like a bunch of red bananas, he ticked off his fingers. 'One: those men have been shot - murder is illegal *here.* Two: they are carrying concealed weapons - also illegal here. Three: they are not in a Diplomatic Corps vehicle. Four: they are parked outside a building where some very important and extremely wealthy people live. Five: they are very dead and are thus causing a public nuisance. Six: they are both visiting foreigners and, even if they *do* happen to be Russian, we don't like visitors being dented while they are here - bad for the tourist trade. You will be able to claim the bodies tomorrow but meantime they are part of my investigation. Now get the hell out of my way and let me get on with my job.'

Leonov, refusing to take no for an answer, persisted but

McLuskey simply ignored him. The Russian, seeing that he was getting nowhere and probably losing considerable face into the bargain, finally sent his ambulance and his people back to the Embassy quarters. He retained only his driver who was also, as it happened, his bodyguard. He had to stay here, had to find out what had happened and, more importantly, why they had been here in the first place. Heaven help them if the British somehow discovered they had been on a murder hunt. Relations between Moscow and this damned Prime Minister were bad enough as it was.

He was still there when the police ambulance drove off with the corpses and the big Ford was towed away. He was also still agitatedly following the Chief Inspector about when two cars arrived from opposite directions. One bore a disgruntled, moody Sir Thomas Griff and the second, a bleary-eyed, half asleep Tim Carter.

Sliding from his car, Griff recognised Carter as he stumbled from his. He waited until the young man joined him under the Bradford awning.

It was a moment before the reporter recognised Sir Thomas under the unfamiliar hat he was wearing. He had met the little man on two previous occasions when Griff had wanted to learn a little more about the HAWL phone calls. Carter was still not quite certain what Griff's interest in the affair was or even who he was. Something to do with security he thought and was intelligent enough to leave well alone. Seeing him now warned the young man that something rather different must have occurred on this occasion. This time too the flat voice on the telephone had simply stated two bodies would be found at the Bradford. No names and no pack drill. On this occasion also, Special Branch had already been alerted before the *Express* warning. Tim sensed a whole new slant to his story as the little man raised his hand in greeting.

'Mr Carter,' the little man said softly, 'a pleasure to see you again. Even if it is at a most unearthly hour.'

Grinning tiredly, Tim shook hands. 'Surprised to see *you* here so quickly, sir.'

Griff shot him a penetrating glance. 'Another telephone call, Tim?'

'Yes, I'm afraid so. I didn't receive it myself, of course, because I was safely home in bed at the time. They played the tape for me though. Same voice, same monotone. Only difference was this time the victims were not named. I thought that was a bit odd, so here I am.'

Griff grasped the reporter's arm firmly and led him to the huge glass doors. The reporter could see a number of people milling about inside. He recognised the massive, beefy figure of Chief Inspector McLuskey.

'Tim,' said Griff, pausing a moment before the gleaming glass. 'This one *is* a bit different. I'm afraid I'm going to have to ask you to keep the lid on it for a while.' He looked up into the reporter's suddenly angry face. 'Now don't get excited until you find out what it's all about. I'm not a great believer in D notices but I think you will find this situation merits one. Now, if you'll take the scowl from your face we'll go inside and find out precisely what has been happening here.'

They pushed the doors wide and stepped into the huge foyer. Almost immediately they were confronted by a large, thickset, heavily jowled man with close cropped hair.

'Sir Thomas,' growled the big man in heavily accented English, 'on behalf of my Government I must lodge the strongest possible protest at the attitude of your police towards this – this unfortunate incident. They are behaving like a bunch of Fascists.'

Griff sighed.

'I'm quite sure you are mistaken, Mr Leonov.' He waved a small hand at Tim Carter. 'May I introduce you to Mr Tim Carter.' He turned his head slightly. 'Tim, this is Mr Anatoli Leonov of the Soviet Embassy. He is – er – the personnel administrator there.'

Tim guessed from the slight hesitation and change of inflection in Griff's voice that whatever Mr Leonov's job might be it was not personnel administration. He decided he had been quietly warned. The big bastard was probably KGB.

The Russian made no effort to shake the reporter's hand. His dark, almost black eyes narrowed thoughtfully. It was obvious to both Englishmen that Leonov had recognised Tim's name and had guessed at the reason for his presence.

Quite suddenly the big man decided to be friendly and belatedly seized the reporter's hand in a bone-crushing grip.

'Ah, the famous Tim Carter of the *Express*,' he chuckled, but there was no mirth in his eyes. 'So you are the man who writes about these terrorists who kill freedom fighters in such a terrible fashion.'

Carter looked at the Russian disbelievingly.

'I wouldn't put it quite that way, Mr Leonov,' he retorted sharply. 'Quite the opposite, in fact.'

The Russian scowled but he had made his point. He turned his attention back to the diminutive Griff.

'You realise, Sir Thomas, the Soviet Union will not appreciate any publicity being given to this matter. I presume you will muzzle your Capitalist Press.'

Griff smiled but his eyes glinted coldly.

'You may presume nothing of the kind, Leonov. Unless, of course, you can tell me why two of your people were armed and precisely what they were doing here.'

The Russian flushed angrily.

'I have already told your damned policemen that I do not know. We can only assume it is some attempt to blacken the character of two Soviet citizens and so besmirch the good standing of the USSR. It is undoubtedly what you and your American blood-brothers would call a frame-up. We Russians do not break the laws of our host countries.'

Carter all but laughed aloud at the utter absurdity of the Russian's little speech. He was beginning to put two and two together and, although the implications gave him a cold feeling in the pit of his stomach, he could see a certain humour in the Russian's attempt to bluster his way out of what was undoubtedly a tough situation. Griff apparently did not share his feelings, however. Carter was amazed, as had been a great many people before him, to see the little man apparently grow in stature as the enormous, driving power bottled inside him blazed to life.

'Since you are apparently in some ignorance, Leonov, let me enlighten you. Your people were attempting to wipe out HAWL before it did too much damage to your damned terrorist network and, hopefully, before it spread its tentacles to other countries.' Carter noticed that Griff had pronounced the word ho-wull. He made a mental note to ask about it. In the meantime he listened as the irate Griff continued to dress down the hulking Russian. 'Now, thanks to your people's ineptness they are very dead and the target probably long gone.

'What you have done is unforgivable in any country. You have alerted HAWL [again Carter noticed the odd pronunciation] to the fact that one of their people may soon be identified. Whatever programme they may have had in mind could now be accelerated, thanks to your stupidity.'

Leonov turned white with anger. Carter had the momentary impression that had the Russian been on his own ground Griff would have been shot out of hand. But the little man was completely undeterred.

'If you are wise, Leonov, you will call off your dogs immediately. For once in your life learn to co-operate or you are just liable to turn loose a force none of us will be able to control.' He turned his head away from the Russian in a gesture of dismissal and for a moment Carter caught the full blaze of the little man's eyes before they hooded themselves and he grinned like a mischievous gnome. 'Come along, young Carter, and we'll see what the police have to tell us.'

The Russian half raised an arm as if he would bar their way but as Griff surged blithely forward it fell limply away and Leonov moved to one side. Tim Carter, his head reeling with the implications of what he had been made privy to, knew he had the story of his life. But he also knew he would never write it.

But Sir Thomas Griff's traumatic Saturday did not end there. Nor, for that matter, did it end for Tim Carter.

Neither man lingered long after the confrontation with the Russian. The police had little to tell them they did not already know. Sir Thomas, realising McLuskey and his men had their own proven methods of getting things done, decided to leave them to it. If a flat had been vacated hastily they would uncover the fact soon enough and inform him immediately. Then, perhaps, they would have some kind of starting point they could be reasonably sure of.

He did not, however, return to the warm bed he had so recently left. Instead the little man went directly to his office thereby also ruining the Saturday of his duty secretary who had been looking forward to a few more peaceful hours.

Tim Carter, by this time well beyond sleep, also, for a reason he would never be certain of, did not return home either. He too, although he had already done his piece for the Sunday edition, elected to give up his Saturday and, to his colleagues' amazement, took his place at his desk.

By 5 a.m. both men somehow became convinced, although there was no obvious reason for it, that they should remain at their desks. Carter and Griff, had they been asked, would undoubtedly have laughed off any suggestion of some form of ESP being at work yet they knew, with almost total conviction, they had to remain at their respective posts. There was, in them both, an ominous sense of foreboding which haunted them through the grim, early morning hours.

Chapter Fifteen

At 8.50 a.m. precisely Tim Carter's telephone rang.

It had also rung thirty minutes previously and he had picked up the instrument with a cold, heavy feeling in the pit of his stomach only to discover his irate wife angrily enquiring as to when she might expect to have the pleasure of her husband's company. He had managed, with the promise of a shopping trip, to mollify her slightly but the call had done little to ease his state of mind. If anything it served only to increase his edginess and caused his colleagues to tread very carefully around his desk space. They recognised the symptoms. Tim Carter's hunches were renowned throughout the huge *Express* building and he was currently displaying, like battle flags, every signal of the malady from his mast head. Consequently, when the telephone sounded its summons for the second time, most heads within earshot turned to watch Carter pick up the instrument as if it were a live coal.

'Tim Carter,' he said quietly, striving to ignore the sick, queasy feeling inside him.

He recognised the voice in his ear immediately. It was not, however, the voice he had been half expecting.

'Morning, Mr Carter, sorr. Pat Scobie here.'

The voice was that of an informer he had used several times while doing a series on the IRA a couple of years before. The man's information had been voluminous and very reliable and the result had been a series which had been well received as being discerning and well informed. It had, in fact, been the turning point in the young reporter's career. Scobie had been very generously remunerated but Carter still felt a sense of obligation to the man. He did not, therefore, cut him off as he might well have done with another caller.

'Yes, Pat. What can I do for you?'

'Well, it's what I can do for you, really. You always treated me well, sorr, and I have a bit o' news might interest ye.'

'OK, Pat, go ahead. What's up?'

There was a momentary pause as if the man on the other end of the line might be having second thoughts about what he was going to say. Then the soft Irish voice resumed.

'Do ye remember me tellin' ye about the Grand Council?'

Carter nodded, remembered he was on the telephone and hastily said, 'Yes.'

'Well, they're meetin' tonight, sorr.'

It was Carter's turn to pause. His mind raced. The Grand Council of the Irish Republican Army was composed of all their senior officers. Because of the very real and obvious dangers the Council met only rarely. This would be the first meeting in several years and could only indicate some kind of crisis within the movement. Carter guessed the crisis would be funds, or, more accurately, the lack of them. What he could not understand was Scobie's reason for calling. The man must have known he was not particularly interested in the movement's problems at the moment - except, perhaps, for one. His heart jolted suddenly and his voice hoarsened.

'Pat, why are you telling me this?'

The Irishman chuckled in his ear. 'Well, Mr Carter, sorr, would ye believe Sean McEwan was a member of the Council?'

In a blinding flash of insight Carter knew what the man was telling him. If Sean McEwan had known of the meeting, then so did HAWL.

'Pat, are you telling me this has been arranged for some time and they haven't changed the venue?'

'They're terrible stubborn men, sorr.'

'Pat,' Carter's excitement was obvious now. His colleagues shrugged and turned back to their own affairs. It looked as if the lucky bastard was on to something again. 'Pat, for Pete's sake, do you know the time and place for the meeting?'

'No, sorr. But I can try to find out.'

'Right, Pat. You do that. I'm coming over on the first available plane. I'll be on the look-out for you at the usual place. And, Pat, thanks a lot.'

'A pleasure, sorr.'

The connection closed and Tim Carter was running to catch his editor before he left the building. Ten minutes later he was talking excitedly to Sir Thomas Griff from the privacy of the editorial office.

Sir Thomas Griff wasted no time. Within ten minutes of receiving Tim Carter's excited call he was talking to what might have been classed as his opposite number in Dublin. Receiving assurances of the Eire Government's co-operation providing they could locate the meeting place and identify the participants Griff then contacted Charles Hamilton and briskly informed him of the situation. Hamilton was immediately perturbed.

'Jesus! You mean those dumb Micks haven't changed their venue?'

'So it would appear, Hamilton,' said Griff curtly. 'Now we know you maintain some kind of contact with these people.' Hamilton started to protest but Griff ran over them. 'I want you to get in touch with your contacts and, if possible, have that meeting stopped.' He could hear the American breathing heavily on the other end of the line and smiled grimly to himself.

'In case you don't think I'm serious, Hamilton, you had better know that HAWL took out two KGB killers last night and Leonov is not exactly deliriously happy about it. If he gets to hear of this he will have so many men over there it will look like a Russian invasion.'

'God Almighty,' yelped the American. 'If that bastard finds out about this there could be all kinds of hell breaking loose over there.'

'Precisely,' the little man said calmly. 'Now, can I rely on your co-operation?'

Suddenly the British were not so bad after all. Hamilton may not have liked them too much but he had virtually been conditioned to hate Russians.

'You're damned right you can, Sir Thomas. I'll see what we can do and come right back to you.'

Griff's third telephone call was to Gerald Parkinson. This was not a particularly easy chore and Sir Thomas wisely left the tracking of the agent to his secretary. She finally tracked him down at Darlington General Hospital. Parkinson's opening remark was disconcerting to the cigar smoking Sir Thomas.

'You must be psychic, sir,' said Gerald tiredly. 'I was just about to call you.'

The little man's cigar twitched like some form of antenna. It was a standing rule that operatives in the field used the telephone to contact their boss as little as possible. Not, as one might assume, for security reasons, but rather that the lines be kept as free as possible for real emergencies. If Parkinson had been about to contact the office then some drastic development had taken place in the North. Griff took a long drag on his cigar.

'What's the problem, Gerald?'

'Fraser's vanished, sir. The police had someone watching him but he's given them the slip. All too easily, I'm afraid.'

Sir Thomas pressed his buzzer for fresh coffee. He did not like the sound of this but somehow, in the light of recent events, he was not particularly surprised.

'When did this happen?'

'That's the problem, sir. We don't know.'

'Explain!'

'Well, sir, Moira - er - Miss Fraser, sir, recovered consciousness about the same time as you and I were talking in the office. Fraser, apparently, had not left her side all night and he remained with her *after* she came round until about lunchtime. It seems he went home then, had a quick meal and a bath, saw the damaged door repaired and the window boarded up, and returned to the hospital for a while. He left there after dark, somewhere around six o'clock the police reckon, saying he was going home to get some sleep. The police followed him there and kept watch on the house all night.'

Parkinson paused a moment then continued.

'When I got back up here I drove out there myself, sir. The

house was in darkness but the police assured me Fraser was still inside. His car was in the garage. Knowing how tired he must have been I decided to leave well alone. Besides, he was, according to the police, securely bottled up. It was a mistake. I should have remembered how Fraser moves in the darkness. He's like a bloody ghost. Could have been breathing down those policeman's necks and they'd never have known he was there.'

Gerald sighed.

'What the police didn't know was Moira, the daughter, sir, also has a car which, because Fraser hadn't had the garage extended yet, she kept in a rented lock-up about quarter of a mile away. He slipped the policemen, took his daughter's car, and vanished. We only discovered this when I went round there just over an hour ago. The police were still guarding an empty house.'

Griff grunted. He was all but hidden in a cloud of smoke.

'So, for all you know, Fraser could have headed straight down here?'

'Yes, sir,' Parkinson's curiosity was aroused. 'What made you say that, sir? Has something else been happening I don't know about?'

Griff's harassed secretary slipped into the room and placed a fresh coffee on the desk. The little man nodded his thanks and quietly informed Parkinson of the KGB killings. Gerald waited until his boss had finished.

'There's a bit more to it than that, isn't there, sir?'

'Yes, I'm afraid there is, Gerald. The killings, of course, are bad enough when you consider the political implications, but I fear we may have another, more immediate problem.' He took the agent carefully through the morning's events. 'So, you see, Gerald I'm not particularly surprised at Fraser's disappearance. If HAWL intend to attack this meeting, and I think it is far too good a target for them to ignore, and *if* Fraser is a part of HAWL then it is a fairly safe bet your man is already in Ireland.

'We have no real idea how many strong this Grand Council will be. At a guess I would put them at around twenty, plus whatever guards they have. Now, HAWL would need to attack that lot in force . . . I can hardly imagine them attempting it with one or two people. Which means they will use every available man they've got and from what you tell me, Fraser would be a definite asset in a situation like this.'

He paused, the tip of his cigar glowing like a fog warning through the smoke.

'Obviously you've been talking to Fraser's daughter, Gerald. Could she shed any light on her father's behaviour?'

'No, sir. I'm afraid not. Fraser apparently told her he'd be gone a few days on business and that she had not to worry. However, I did gather he has been behaving fairly erratically over the past week or two. You know, staying away overnight and that sort of thing.

'She knows it isn't women, sir. She could understand that but apparently Fraser is the original one woman man, and his wife was that woman. It's been worrying her quite a lot apparently, because she feels Fraser may be hankering after going back to soldiering and is trying to arrange a new contract.

'That could well be true, sir. But one of his trips coincides with the Roseford killings.'

Sir Thomas did not particularly like the way things appeared to be working out. In his view when things began to add up easily he was working on the wrong sum. Still, there seemed little doubt Fraser could be one of their men. Now they had to find him before he got close to that damned meeting.

'Right, Gerald,' he said decisively. 'You'll have to get yourself across to Ireland. I've already arranged for you to tie up with Tim Carter and his informant. We may be pursuing a very forlorn hope but at least you'll be able to recognise Fraser if you see him. When you get over there, keep in touch with me on an hourly basis. That way I'll be able to relay information to you almost as fast as I get it.

'Now. What about the girl – er – Moira? Is she fit to travel?'

'Yes, sir. The hospital intend to release her this morning. Apparently her X-rays came up clear. Her head might ache a little for a couple of days but that will be it.'

'Good! Arrange a plain clothes escort for her and fly her down here. Don't take no for an answer. With the Russians, and Heaven alone knows who else involved, we can't afford to take chances. I want her down here where I can keep an eye on her. And, Gerald – '

'Yes, sir?'

'Watch your back.'

Chapter Sixteen

Three times in the course of the day he drove past the house. Never too fast and never slow enough that his progress might excite attention. Each time he used a different car and each time his appearance had been subtly altered to escape recognition by the sharp-eyed guards on the gate who were supposed to be trimming the edge of the drive. Twice, armed with a pair of high-powered binoculars, he had wandered to the top of a nearby hill and unobtrusively studied the house and its grounds.

All in all, he had made four trips to the area since the Roseford operation. On three of those occasions he had wandered unhindered through the grounds until he had become familiar with the terrain and the layout of the gardens. On the last occasion he had come like a thief in the night and had wandered repeatedly through the twenty rooms of the Manor House. On this occasion, he had not, like a thief, removed some of the contents but had brought, instead, a number of rather odd items, which he had carefully concealed in various places throughout the old house.

Fairlee Manor lay in County Westmeath and, not too far from Lough Ennell, was a particularly lonely place. At one time it had been the home of lesser English gentry with more money than good sense who had dabbled, not too successfully, in horse breeding. But today it was owned by a writer who had used it as a tax haven. The writer had suddenly struck it big with a bestseller and immediately fled to the United States to make it even bigger by writing for movies. He had, it seemed, all but forgotten his Irish home because he had not been near the place in two years, much to the gratification of the ancient caretaker and the great glee of the IRA who used it frequently.

The rolling acreage over which the original owner's horses had galloped was gone now of course but the eight or nine acres which had been the home grounds remained. Grounds a little tatty and overgrown now perhaps but still surrounded by a solid, eight foot high stone wall breached by a single large and fiendishly ornate gateway opening directly on to the drive. The house itself was an almost square, two storey structure squatting, like a large grey sugar cube, in the middle of its unkept lawns and disused tennis courts.

The Manor, from the IRA's point of view, had several advantages for illicit meetings. The first, of course, was its extreme isolation, the nearest village being four miles away. The second was that the author, when he had been only middling-wealthy, had installed his own diesel-fuelled power plant producing power at the turn of a key. Its size also made it particularly useful, its many rooms being able to shelter considerable numbers of men without presenting too many problems. Lastly, with its solid, undamaged surrounding wall, it was relatively easily guarded.

As he drove past for the third and last time he was fairly well satisfied with his preparations. He had a clear map of the entire grounds in his head, his access point was already prepared, and he had finally established there would be four guards. Two on the gate and two patrolling the grounds. There was no sign of any dogs and the caretaker had vanished from the scene in his creaking old Austin hours ago. All he had to do now was wait.

Tim Carter and Gerald Parkinson were slowly but surely becoming more and more discouraged. The odds against them finding the venue for the Grand Council meeting were becoming longer and longer. Twice so far Pat Scobie had slipped into the bar, joined them for a quick beer, reported negative results, and sidled out again. Both men had, for a while, made a little desultory conversation but even that had waned considerably and they spent long silent periods simply staring into their beer glasses as they waited for news that they were beginning to believe would never come.

The cocktail bar of the Shamrock Hotel on the outskirts of Dublin was not, in the off-peak season, exactly a hive of activity and the pair were alone (save for the occasional appearance of a flirtatious little barmaid who seemed to have something going for her in the kitchen) in its red imitation leather and stainless steel opulence. They had elected to book rooms in the place figuring that if nothing else it would serve them as a base to operate from.

Carter, his long night beginning to catch up with him, slipped gradually into a soporific state and was only prevented from falling asleep over the bar by the sudden reappearance of the barmaid.

'Would either of you gentlemen be Mr Parkinson?' she asked, fluttering her eyelashes and flashing them a smile which promised immediate access to the Kingdom of Heaven. Parkinson acknowledged himself and she reached under the bar and produced a telephone. 'There's a call for you, sir.'

Gerald picked up the receiver.

'Gerald?' The musical baritone of Sir Thomas Griff sounded clearly in his ear.

'Yes, sir?'

'Call me back, please.'

The connection closed immediately but, for the benefit of the bright little barmaid, Gerald continued to listen intently to the empty hum on the line for a few moments longer. Presently he said, 'Five hundred pairs, sir? I'll see to it,' winked at the barmaid and replaced the receiver.

Tim, alerted now and more or less awake, sipped thoughtfully at his drink until the barmaid, with a grand display of her pneumatic upperworks, replaced the telephone under the bar and vanished once more into the nether regions.

'What's up?'

'Don't know yet,' grunted Parkinson. 'I'll have to call him from one of the payphones out in the foyer. Hang on here. I'll be straight back.'

He got through to the little man immediately. The telephone was picked up on the first ring.

'Gerald?'

'Yes, sir.'

Sir Thomas wasted no time. Gerald, sensing the urgency, did not interrupt.

'The CIA have come up with a possible venue. They can't guarantee it but it's the best they can do in the time they had. They seem to think it might be held in a place called Fairlee Manor. That's in Westmeath, and, as far as I can gather, roughly sixty miles from where you are now.' Gerald smiled at this. The little man could probably have told him the exact distance to within a couple of hundred yards.

'I'm afraid you're on your own with this, Gerald. The CIA are slightly in the huff and are holding off and the Eire Government have suddenly decided to throw up all kinds of objections although they will go conveniently blind for twenty-four hours.

'If this Fairlee Manor turns out to be the venue then it's going to be tough. There is just no way I can get help to you in time. Even if I could get some SAS people down there you would probably be long gone before they could get to you. Maybe you can get some help from Carter - he seems to be a good lad - but in any case I'm telling you not to try and be a hero. *Don't* get involved unless you have no alternative. If you can get any kind of make on these HAWL people that will be good enough. Do you understand me?'

'Yes, sir.'

'Right! Now I've arranged for some - er - extra comfort for you. It should arrive at the hotel in about twenty minutes or so. But see if you can manage without it, will you? Now have you got all that?'

'Yes. Quite clear, sir.'

'Good luck, Gerald.'

The connection closed. Parkinson slid out of the booth and returned to the bar.

He had watched them trickle slowly into the manor. One at a time, with anything up to an hour between them, they arrived in a variety of conveyances which deposited their passengers and left immediately. There was going to be no build-up of parked vehicles to warn the casual passer-by that something was afoot. As dusk closed in upon the land he calculated at least seven members of the Grand Council had so far arrived. Before he left his vantage point to set about his own preparations he noted the lights of two more vehicles enter and leave the grounds.

As he walked briskly around the dark green, letterless van carefully parked and concealed well off the road, he was not to know the nine members of the Council now present in the manor would be all who would come. Four were already dead, three by his own hand and the fourth a victim of Seamus O'Malley's fear. Two were serving twenty-year sentences in the Maze prison and another was slowly dying of cancer. The remaining twelve, with a healthy regard for their own skins, had decided that with the possibility of HAWL being aware of the meeting, Fairlee Manor was not where they wanted to be.

Had he been aware of all this it would have made no difference. The attack had been planned, the groundwork done, and time was not on his side. Had the manor contained only a single Council member the operation would go ahead as planned. Terror was rebounding upon those who used it on the innocents.

The youthful messenger delivered the carefully sealed package to Parkinson's room half an hour after the agent had completed his call to Griff. Gerald tipped the round-faced lad with a pound note as he accepted the package. The boy's delighted whistle was clearly audible through the door as Gerald closed it carefully behind him. Weighing the package carefully in his hands Parkinson turned towards Tim Carter.

'If you want to back out, Tim, this is your last chance.'

Carter, his back to the window, buttocks firmly planted on the sill, shook his head and eyed the package curiously. He could see the printed labels quite clearly. 'Lacey's Lingerie' they read, with Parkinson's name and room number scrawled in a heavy black hand. Now Tim understood Parkinson's odd statement about five hundred pairs into a dead telephone. Obviously the hard-looking young policeman, secret agent, or whatever the hell he was, was supposed to be some kind of lingerie salesman. Which, to Tim's mind, was a piss-poor piece of casting. He could imagine Gerald dealing with lingerie in one way only. But then he had never seen Parkinson at his charming best. Of one thing Carter was certain, however. Whatever that package contained, it was *not* five hundred pair of ladies' knickers.

'No,' Carter said slowly, 'for better or worse I'm in this thing now. I've come this far and I'll be damned if I'm going to back out now. Besides' – he grinned disarmingly – 'I learned long ago when to keep my head down.'

Parkinson studied him thoughtfully for a moment then, chuckling, quietly stripped the bright wrapping from the package revealing an expensive looking cardboard box over-printed endlessly with the 'Lacey's Lingerie' legend. Laying the box on the bed he lifted the lid. Tim came off the window sill and peered curiously down into the box.

The reporter felt vaguely disappointed.

The box was packed to the brim with cellophane packets, each packet containing a pair of what was undoubtedly the tiniest, flimsiest panties the reporter had ever clapped eyes on. In a wide variety of colours they seemed, to his bemused eyes, to glow with vaguely sexy reproval against the slightly off-white bedcover. Grinning widely at the expression on the reporter's face Parkinson swept several layers of the tiny packets carelessly to one side. In a violent cascade of colour they spread over the bed and tumbled, sparkling to the floor.

Tim Carter, however, was unaware of the kaleidoscopic effect of Parkinson's ruthless digging. His eyes were focussed entirely on the sinister outlines of two Scorpion VZ61 machine pistols. Wire butts neatly folded over the barrels, they glinted with a dull, obscene lustre against the garish rainbow of the panties.

Chapter Seventeen

Carrying his awkward bundle in his right hand and holding it well clear of his body and the wall, the lithe, black, almost formless shadow agilely mounted the eight-foot lightweight aluminium ladder leaning against the damp stone. The ladder, painted a dull, matt black reflected none of what little light seeped through heavy, hanging clouds. It sprung very slightly as the man's weight was removed and he gained the top of the wall.

Pausing, like a huge cat on the wall coping, the intruder listened carefully to the murmurings of the night.

Vaguely, seeming little more than extra sighs from the wind as it soughed through the bare boughs of the trees, he could hear the muted sound of conversation from the gate to the North of him. Satisfied his timing had been reasonably accurate, the shadowy figure fumbled a moment with the misshapen bundle. Freeing a length of strong nylon cord attached to it, he carefully lowered the bundle to the ground on the inside of the wall. As the bundle finally came to rest he dropped the cord softly behind it.

Again he listened carefully to the night. Satisfied there had been no change to the status quo the strange, black figure flickered from the top of the wall and retraced his steps.

Moving swiftly, but with a silence incredible for his bulk, he slipped through a tangled mass of gorse and whin to where the dark bulk of the van was hidden. So well concealed was the vehicle that he almost missed it in the darkness and had to change direction slightly. He made a mental note of this. It was a point he would do well to remember when the job was done.

At the van he wasted no time but worked swiftly and methodically. First he donned a flat topped, dark visored hood which spread out from his neck and over his shoulders like a cape, then buckled a soft leather belt tightly around his black overalled waist. The belt, among other things, supported two sheathed, black bladed, commando type daggers on his right hip and a holstered Walther P38 on his left. The butt of the P38 faced forward to facilitate a fast, cross body draw. At the back of the belt, held in place by a press stud toggle, hung the twin handles of a wire garrotte.

After tugging at the buckle once or twice to test it for security, the hooded figure performed a few quick, twisting movements as if he were executing some kind of modern dance. Satisfied that none of his weaponry had collided and produced a noise he slung a Kalashnikov across his chest from a peculiar, black, specially fabricated sling. The sling was made in three separate compartments held together by burr fasteners. A single sharp tug and the weapon would be free with two short lengths of sling still dangling from it and the third remaining suspended round his neck. He tested the sling once and grunted in satisfaction at the speed with which the weapon slipped into his hands.

The Kalashnikov securely back in place, he performed his ritual twist once more. Again he could hear no tell-tale chink. Satisfied at last, he picked up yet another oddly shaped bundle and headed back through the grasping tangle toward the wall.

Safely inside the perimeter and working by touch alone, he unpacked the bundles and began to assemble his equipment, taking great care that no single piece of metal accidentally struck another. Sound travels a fair distance at night and he had no great wish to alarm the guards. A hundred times he had rehearsed this moment until he could strip and assemble the thing with his eyes closed, which, to all intents and purposes, he was virtually doing now.

He froze for a second, then recovered.

Slowly, with infinite care, he placed the piece of equipment on which he had been working gently on the damp earth before him. Making no sudden movements he reached up and pulled the caped hood free of his head and laid it on the ground also. The cold air stung his overheated face sharply and he shivered slightly.

His face a pallid grey blob floating in inky shadow, he turned his head slightly and sniffed the air like an animal. He caught it again almost immediately: the same sharp, pungent odour which had filtered into his hood. Burning tobacco! Someone was smoking a cigarette close by.

Moving like a wraith, the silent, almost formless figure flitted from tree to tree seeking the source of the odour. Merging with the looming bulk of a rough-barked oak he caught the glowing arc of the cigarette as it was lifted to its owner's mouth. The man was little more than twenty feet away, leaning against the bole of another tree. The guard drew on his cigarette. His hard, unshaven face glowed redly for a second and instantly something hissed softly in the air.

The long bladed commando knife took him cleanly in the throat. The burning cigarette leaped away from his mouth in a crazy, spinning arc as he made a little coughing sound and clawed at his neck. His hand encountered and grasped the hilt of the knife. A hand crushed over his mouth and an iron band clamped around his wrist. The guard's hand, still grasping the hilt of the knife, was wrenched savagely across his face. The razor sharp blade ripped open his throat and, in a wet gouting rush of warm blood, he died.

'Thomas, where the fuck are yez, man?'

The harsh, Belfast accented voice was close. Too close. It was the second of the two-man patrolling guard. Retrieving his knife, the intruder flung the still quivering body away from him. It thudded to the ground with a sound like a dumped sack of wet flour.

'Jezus! What the . . . ?'

The second guard rushed forward out of the night. The intruder caught the pale blob of his face and, like an uncoiling spring, he came up out of a half-crouch and smashed savagely into the bulk of the oncoming man. The guard's breath exploded in a harsh, sobbing gasp. He was aware of a secondary punching blow just below his ribcage. Then nothing.

Quickly the black clad man removed his knife from the corpse, sheathed it with its mate, and returned silently to his work. If anything, he worked slightly faster than before. It would not be too long before the men at the gate noticed the absence of the other pair. The job had to be done before they realised something was wrong and alerted the house. He would deal with the guards later.

Joe Boyd was sadly disappointed at the failure of the Council to appear. Nine from a total of twenty-eight could hardly be called a full meeting. True, four were dead, one nearly so, and two in prison, but one of the items on the agenda had been to vote in new members to replace the missing seven. They could hardly do that now, of course, since it needed unanimous agreement to elect a candidate. Not, he thought bitterly, that they'd all that damned many eligible men left to choose from.

He supposed it was the HAWL thing which was keeping them away. The absentees were all people who had advocated a change of venue, arguing that a new place should be found – one that HAWL could not possibly know about. He had resisted this strongly. After all, they were the Provisionals, the real fighting men of the Republic. Why should they hide themselves from something they knew damn all about? Besides, hadn't this place been tried and proven many times? With the gates closed and locked and four armed men patrolling the grounds not even a bloody ghost could get near them. Anyway, he still wasn't certain that HAWL was not something dreamed up by the English to scare the Bejezus out of them.

He looked round the table at the eight hard-eyed men who were seated with him and all but laughed. Jesus, if that writer fellow only knew what his dining room was being used for. Him being an Englishman, he would likely throw a dozen kind of fits. Before calling the meeting to order he glanced instinctively at the heavy velvet drapes drawn across the long mullioned windows. Aye, they were all right. There would be damned little light showing from the outside.

In the instant before Boyd took his eyes from the closed drapes something solid thrown from outside shattered a window and billowed out the curtains. Before the startled men had time, either to rise to their feet or reach for their weapons, the huge room was suddenly filled with glaring white light as an incandescent stream of liquid flame hosed into the room and splashed across the table to spatter over the shocked Council.

Immediately the meeting became a screaming, burning shambles as men, their clothes and hair flaming, shrieked in terrible agony and fought to smother flames which stuck to their flesh and somehow continued to burn. Two, screaming like demented souls and their arms flailing wildly, made it to the door in the same instant as thermite bombs placed beneath the floorboards all over the house reacted to a radio impulse and exploded into white-hot fury. They were lucky, and died immediately as flame seared into their lungs. The men in the dining room were not so lucky. Those still alive made terrible, agonised sounds, inhuman in their terrified torture, and blundered blindly about the chamber, groping blindly for an exit as they struggled to cling to life even at its tormented worst.

From somewhere outside another incandescent flood poured into the room and in a moment the shrieking stopped.

The two guards on the gate, immediately alarmed by the screaming of burning men and the muffled, thudding explosions of the thermite bombs, raced across the lawns to the house. The old building was already an inferno. Even as they sped towards it the guards knew there was going to be nothing they could do, but with the blind, stubborn courage of the Irish they were intent on trying. Eyes fixed on the burning building neither man was aware of the weird, misshapen, space suited figure standing slightly to the right of the doomed manor.

The first either man was to know of the alien presence was when a white, brilliant streak of flame left it and arced towards them.

The white hot curve of molten fire appeared to swoop down upon them in some horrible form of slow motion yet they were aware they were powerless to avoid it. Suddenly the falling fire appeared to accelerate. They were engulfed in searing flame which ignited their clothing, immediately removed every vestige of hair from their heads and began to burn into living flesh with an intensity which set their own fat burning. Screaming in unimaginable agony the burning men careered about the lawn while the intense heat exploded the cartridges in their discarded Armalites.

The man in the cumbersome hood and the awkward-looking back pack carrying a tank unit turned a valve with a thick, asbestos gloved hand. The tiny blue light of the flame thrower's pilot light extinguished immediately. The eyes behind the dark visor watched the screaming, horrifying dance of the burning guards coldly. Once his hand moved as if to free the Kalashnikov across his chest and end their agony. But the movement was not carried through. One behind the other the shrieking men collapsed, writhing and burning, on the damp grass.

Slowly, almost wearily, the intruder shrugged the cumbersome pack from his shoulders and set it on the ground. Then, possibly with an increasing sense of urgency, he stripped off the bulky firefighter's hood and coveralls and tossed them beside his discarded equipment and gloves. Once more in his black, almost skintight overalls, he replaced his Kalashnikov and weapons belt and, with a last look at the inferno he had created, loped away with the easy, relaxed strides of an athlete.

Behind him the two smouldering guards were still. His abandoned equipment, illuminated clearly in the flickering glare, lay where it would be found easily. Along the upper face of the squat-looking tank the neatly painted letters HAWL glowed with an eerie red light.

Parkinson, racing the hired Rover along narrow Irish roads, knew they were too late when Carter drew his attention to the flickering red glow on the horizon. But even so he was not prepared for the devastation which met their eyes as they crested a small hill and looked down on the burning manor. The fire was just passing its peak. The roof had collapsed but the timber, drying for over a hundred years, burned viciously within the gutted shell, sending great leaping flames shooting ten to twelve feet above what had been the level of the eaves.

'Christ,' said Carter in an awed voice. 'If the Council were in there none of them can be alive. Nothing could survive *that*.'

Parkinson nosed the car up to the massive, closed gates. Scrambling out of the car he pushed at the heavy ironwork.

'You could be right, Tim,' he said as Carter came up behind him. 'I don't think any of them got out. This gate is locked and there is no sign of any guards. Either HAWL have torched an empty house or they've wiped out the entire bunch including the guards. We'd better find out and get the hell out of here. This place will be alive with people shortly.'

Stepping off from the bonnet of the Rover, they clambered over the gate and raced towards the burning house. Almost immediately they all but stumbled across the two naked, blackened and still smoking bodies of the guards. A strong stench which reminded Carter of roast pork hung over the contorted lumps of carbon. He threw up immediately.

'What a horrible fucking way to die,' he gasped, wiping his mouth with a trembling hand. 'Nobody deserves to die like that.'

Parkinson seized his arm and all but dragged him to the discarded pile of equipment.

'Save your sympathy for the people these bastards have killed and injured. For my money they got what's been coming to them for years.' He kicked the squat tank gently as Carter took in the neatly printed letters. 'Flame thrower. No doubt about who used it either. HAWL just walked in here and fried the lot of them like so many sausages. Come on, we've got all we need to know.'

Carter hung back slightly.

'Aren't you going to have a look around? Some of the HAWL people may still be somewhere about.'

Parkinson rounded on him angrily.

'You're talking like a bloody idiot, Tim.' He waved his hand towards the blazing house. 'Don't you think they will realise this is acting like a beacon? HAWL will be long gone and we'd better get moving too or we'll be trying to answer some bloody awkward questions. The Irish are a long way from being as daft as the jokes would have you believe. Now, let's get the hell out of here.'

Chapter Eighteen

'Gerald, let's just sit a moment and put together what we've got so far.' Sir Thomas Griff, his grey hair wreathed in smoke like cloud hanging around a mountain top, leaned forward across his desk and addressed Gerald Parkinson. 'Somewhere in all of this there is a pattern - a grand design if you like. I think if we pause long enough and mull things over a little that pattern may become evident.'

Parkinson eased himself back in his chair, crossed his legs and generally made himself comfortable. He knew there was no need for comment. His chief was simply about to use him as a sounding board. He had seen the little man in this mood many times in the past and it never failed to amaze him how he could pull together apparently unrelated facts and begin to form them into a composite picture. The process invariably fascinated him.

He had come straight to the office from the airport to be debriefed and this was the culmination. Something he had said had obviously triggered Griff's amazingly complex mind and he was being allowed to hear the little man put the pieces together.

The story, as seen through Tim Carter's eyes, had, of course, already made headlines in the Sunday edition. Over and above Tim's story (telephoned from Dublin), the *Express* had received its usual call from HAWL giving them the names of all but two of the men who had perished in the manor. Formal identification, according to the Eire police, would probably be next to impossible and they were working on the assumption that the *Express* information was correct. The identity of the guards was also being established. The seven men named were wanted by the police on both sides of the border and had as much Irish blood as British on their hands. There had been no mention of the killing of the two Russians.

'We are assuming, I think correctly, that HAWL has been created for the purpose of bringing terror home to the terrorists. What brought this about could be any one of dozens of terror attacks but we assume, and again I believe we are right, that the Granada Bomb incident was the actual spark. What we don't know is how long HAWL have been planning this campaign. Was it a long time before the Granada incident? Or did it all actually begin from that point?

'I believe the Granada atrocity was the trigger. So, obviously, do the Americans and the Russians. Taking that as a starting point are we really to believe a new group has been formed, trained, thrown into action, in less than a year?

'I think not!

'Now, what does that leave us with?'

Gerald made no attempt to answer. He was not expected to. Taking another reflective puff at his fiercely burning Napoleon the older man answered his own question.

'It leaves us with the possibility that some person, very likely a survivor or a bereaved relative, finally snapped. It's something which has always been on the cards because it is part of what terrorism is really all about. Terrorists aim to destroy the rule of law for their own ends. They *want* to bring killing into the streets. However, with HAWL it seems to have backfired. With the exception of the two Russians the HAWL killings have been confined to terrorists which is *not* part of the plan.

'Accepting the fact HAWL could be a one-person show we have to consider if a woman could have committed the killings. The answer, I think, would have to be no. It took pure brute strength to hoist O'Mannion up that lamppost and remove Riordan from his bed. A woman, of course, could be capable of it but I think the possibility is remote. Therefore we are left with a man. A powerful man with at least a nodding acquaintance with Arabic and trained to kill.

'However,' the little man waved his cigar in Gerald's general direction like a conductor admonishing his lead violin, 'to conduct a campaign such as this requires two things apart from the ability to kill. It requires a considerable amount of brain power and it needs an awful lot of money.

'So, with this possibility in mind I had our police friends take a look at the priorities on our list. Presumably after having terrorised a few bank managers they have discovered that nobody on our list comes anywhere near the wealthy bracket. Your friend Fraser could be classified as 'comfortable' but he would be the only one. His bank balance, however, is remarkably static – no big withdrawals whatsoever.

'But some bright spark over at the Yard suddenly remembered a spate of one-man robberies which took place shortly after the Granada affair. *All* the robberies appear to have been planned with military precision and *all* were successful with nobody hurt.'

The smoke cloud hovering around Griff thickened visibly as he warmed to his theory. Gerald struggled to prevent himself from coughing.

'Now we both know it is a classical terrorist tactic to rob banks and payrolls in order to finance their operations. HAWL appears to have the ability to think like a terrorist therefore this method of raising funds will not have escaped his attention. Witnesses claim the robber was a big man, but not a huge man as Fraser appears to be. Since, as the police point out, any man with a gun in his hands appears much larger than life to terrified witnesses, they are assuming him to be anything from five foot nine to six foot.'

The little man stopped in mid-flow and grinned impishly at his agent.

'Are you with me so far, Gerald?'

Parkinson stirred slightly. For some reason he felt oddly relieved that Moira Fraser's father appeared, for the moment, to be reasonably free of suspicion, although he undoubtedly had a great deal of explaining to do. He cleared his throat roughly.

'Er – yes, sir. I think so.'

'Well, what do you think?'

Parkinson groaned inwardly. This was not usually a part of Griff's theorising. Something had to be troubling him about it and he wanted to see if his subordinate could come up with the same thing. Gerald's not inconsiderable intellect raced into top gear.

'Well, sir,' he said slowly, 'I agree it's possible we could be dealing with one man. But if you look at what's been done, you have to admit it appears a bit unlikely. If we accept the theory, then he tackled, single-handed, three armed and very dangerous men at Roseford Farm; wiped out *and* tortured Sadiq Ali Qadar in a busy hotel in broad daylight; took O'Mannion, also armed, in a Dublin Street, lifted Riordan from his bed; killed two trained and armed Russians; and then, finally, last night's episode!'

'Well, how about last night?'

Parkinson momentarily wished he were elsewhere.

'Damn it, sir, the Provos knew it was on the cards HAWL would come after them. Yet they didn't change the meeting place. The whole damned thing could have been a set-up. When they guessed HAWL knew about the meeting they could have turned it into a trap. In fact, I still can't understand why they didn't. HAWL must have known they could be lying in wait. Only a raving lunatic would have attempted to go in there alone. Either that or – or – ' His voice tailed away as another thought struck him.

Griff's eyes were suddenly sharp.

'Or what, Gerald?'

'Or else it was done by somebody who just didn't care whether they lived or died.'

Sir Thomas blew a long stream of smoke across the desk.

'Precisely, Gerald. You've hit the nail right on the head. But where does this suicidal attitude come from? The psychology of this man is important and it's one of the things we have to worry about if we are to stop him. Is all this because HAWL thinks he had nothing left to live for? Is it some form of religious mania? Does he believe, for example, he has been chosen to rid the world of terrorism? Or is he simply imbued with some form of blind hate which leads him to ignore personal danger?'

Griff coughed slightly and glared angrily at his half-smoked Napoleon as if defying it to induce another spasm.

'Or,' he continued with a slightly injured look, 'is it some peculiar amalgam of all three which motivates our man? Something which you and I, in our state of conditioned sanity, simply cannot understand?'

Laying his cigar on the edge of a large glass ashtray Griff steepled his fingers in another gesture which Gerald knew well. Some aspect of his own theory still troubled the little man. He waited to discover what it might be.

Parkinson was destined not to learn what troubled Sir Thomas, however, because at that moment the intercom buzzed apologetically. Griff leaned forward and depressed a button exasperatedly.

'Yes, Miss Carter?'

'It's Miss *Alexander*, sir.' Griff could never remember which name belonged to which secretary. 'I have Professor Hughes here, sir. He says he may have something of importance to tell you.'

Griff clicked his tongue with uncharacteristic impatience.

'Oh dear! Tell him I'm – er – no! Send him in please.'

Presently, with the introductions over and Hughes comfortably seated with, to Parkinson's cringing dismay, a Napoleon going at full blast, Griff addressed the reason for the Professor's unexpected visit.

'Mr – er – Professor Hughes, I believe you think you may have something important to tell us.'

Hughes looked vaguely embarrassed for a moment and eyed his cigar reflectively as if wondering whether his information were worthy of Griff's munificence.

'Well, I – ah – I only believe it's important because it has been troubling me for some time. It was the reports of this new Irish incident which triggered me and I suddenly recalled what had been bothering me.'

Griff nodded sagely as if he knew exactly what the linguist was talking about. Encouraged by the little man's attentiveness Hughes ploughed ahead.

'As I told you on my last visit the word *hawl* is Arabic for terror,' he cleared his throat nervously. 'However, I omitted to tell you an extension of this is the term *abu hawl* or, if you like, "father of terror". This term is applied by the Arabs mainly to the Sphinx.'

Griff blinked. Parkinson concealed a smile.

'I don't quite see wh – '

Hughes raised his hand as if he were curbing an over-enthusiastic student. Griff, to Parkinson's astonishment, subsided. Hughes continued urbanely.

'Do either of you know the Greek legend of the Sphinx?'

Gerald laughed.

'I guess most people do, Professor. Something to do with it asking travellers a riddle of some kind. If they couldn't come up with the correct answer then it killed and ate them.'

'Quite right, Mr Parkinson,' said Hughes happily. Gerald had the feeling he had just received the equivalent of a pat on the head. 'Legend has it the Sphinx lived outside the city of Thebes and asked all passers-by this riddle: what has a single voice and yet becomes four-footed, two-footed and three-footed? Oedipus, on his way to the city, was asked the riddle and infuriated the Sphinx by answering it immediately. He said it was – '

'A man!' Griff interjected.

Hughes blinked happily through his spectacles.

'Ah. So you are familiar with the legend also, Sir Thomas?'

Griff, his small, neat fingers busy with the wrapper of yet another Napoleon, shook his head.

'No. But I think I'm beginning to see your drift, Professor.'

'Quite, quite,' gurgled Hughes. 'The answer, man, is quite correct because when he is young he walks on hands and feet, on two feet for most of his life, and with the assistance of a cane or stick when he is old. Now this leads me to believe that perhaps you might not be looking for an organisation but for a solitary man.'

Griff's luminous eyes caught Parkinson's for a moment. Hughes burbled happily on.

'Of course the Greek Sphinx began to occur in fairly recent times, around 1500 BC. But it had existed in Egypt for over a thousand years before that. In fact, the oldest, and, of course the most famous example, is *abu hawl*, better known as the

Great Sphinx of Giza which is thought to have been built around 2500 BC during the reign of King Khafre.'

'*Who*?' Again Griff interrupted.

Hughes was momentarily flustered.

'Ah – Khafre, King Khafre.'

'Could you spell that please?'

'Certainly: K-H-A-F-R-E.'

'But you pronounce it "Kaffray"?'

Hughes was now completely bewildered.

'Ah – yes, I believe so. Is it important?'

Griff smiled. His eyes appeared to have gained greater brillance and a bemused Gerald Parkinson guessed his boss was on to something. Sir Thomas's next statement confirmed this.

'Very important indeed, Professor. You are, in fact, being of enormous help to us. Please continue.'

Gratified Hughes beamed through the tobacco haze.

'Actually there isn't very much more really. It is, of course, fairly generally believed that the Sphinx is supposed to represent the god Horus who had the job of guarding temples and tombs.' He blinked apologetically. 'At this point gentlemen, I have to become a little fanciful I'm afraid.'

'Go ahead, Professor, please,' Griff waved his cigar gently in the air. 'I'm finding all this of great interest.'

Hughes took a defensive puff at his cigar then plunged headlong on.

'Well, having got so far with my *abu hawl* idea I now became slightly bogged down. Assuming that I was right and that the word *hawl* was being used for two purposes, that is to strike terror and also to provide a clue that only a single man was involved; I then had to wonder what this single man, or Horus, if you like, was supposed to be guarding.' He grinned a trifle sheepishly. 'I was trying to follow my idea through to the bitter end, you see.'

Griff nodded encouragingly.

'I understand. Go ahead, please.'

'Horus, you see, as I previously mentioned, is supposed to be the guardian of temples. Now what temple could he be guarding in my context? It took me quite a long time before I had it. HAWL, gentlemen, is looking at the innocents who suffer through terrorism. Families broken by bereavement and injury.

'The family, generally speaking, is a sacrosanct entity to the majority of men. He will brook no interference with it and he will, and does, fight and die to protect it. The family, if you like is a form of temple – the Temple of Man.'

Half an hour later, a beaming Hughes, two boxes of Griff's precious Napoleons tucked under his arm, was personally escorted to the door by an equally beaming Sir Thomas. The little man practically skipped back to his desk and immediately pressed his call button for coffee.

'Now, Gerald, we really have to get down to some hard work. Our delightful Professor Hughes has filled in some gaps for me, but, better still, he has given us a lead.'

Parkinson blinked.

'I'm afraid I don't follow you, sir. It all seemed more than a little airy-fairy to me.'

Griff twinkled at him like a mischievous leprechaun. He tapped a folder on his desk.

'Ah, but you see, Gerald, you have not yet seen the list of residents at Bradford Tower. Among them you will find a certain Mr Anthony Kaffray. This gentleman, it would appear, is very much conspicuous by his absence.'

Chapter Nineteen

Anne Parkinson stared at her brother in shocked disbelief.

'I don't believe it,' she said finally. 'It's absolutely impossible! He – he's too sick. There's just no way he could have done those terrible things.'

Gerald Parkinson's eyes softened as he looked down into his sister's stricken face.

'Anne,' his voice was gentle. 'I know you have a bit of a soft spot for him, but,' he indicated a thick buff folder lying on the arm of Anne's chair, 'you've just read his file. He's not a name on a computer printout any longer. That's his life, the complete man. I know it's difficult for you to reconcile all you've just read with the broken-down hulk you see him as but, according to the record, he could well have been a first class actor had he wanted to go that way. Most of his college life he was involved, deeply involved, with amateur theatricals. And what about that spell of his in Ireland? Dammit, he was so good at it the police were constantly locking him up. The SAS say he was one of the very few they never worried about and they, obviously, were not talking purely about his acting ability.'

Anne, her face chalk-white, tried vainly to reconcile the shy, ill, all but broken man she had dined with and the highly efficient killing machine outlined in the dossier. Her heart told her it was impossible but a coldly analytical part of her mind kept churning the indisputable facts over and over. Gerald, guessing at what she was going through, wisely kept his mouth shut.

It had been only two hours before the results of several strongly worded telephone calls from the Home Secretary had arrived, via various couriers, on Griff's desk. The little man, convinced, apparently, that one of their top six suspects had to be HAWL, had exerted enough pressure to have several highly inflammable dossiers released to his care. It had taken two days to pry the files loose from jealous officialdom even with Home Office approval. The dossiers had been much as expected save that of Captain William Wilkinson who, although apparently with the Royal Engineers, had been a member of the SAS for no less than ten years.

It had been Wilkinson's record in Ulster which had made Griff and Parkinson sit up and take notice. The man had been alone, undercover, in largely hostile territory for almost fourteen months. During this time he had been responsible for some twenty arrests. He had posed, all that time, as an apparently harmless alcoholic. He had also served in Oman and possessed more than a passing familiarity with Arabic. He was classified as an excellent soldier which was an SAS euphemism for 'highly dangerous'.

Which was why, for the first time in his career, Gerald had, with Griff's approval, brought a top secret file home from the office and shown it to his sister. Anne had shown no surprise on learning of Gerald's activities, having long since been aware he was not the desk-bound civil servant he purported to be. She had, in fact, several times visited him in hospital when he had been suffering from wounds not inflicted by falling off his chair. She had, however, been startled and not a little frightened by his suspicions concerning Bill Wilkinson.

She shook her auburn head.

'I - I still can't believe it, Gerry. He's such a nice man.'

Her brother smiled sympathetically.

'I know how you feel, Anne. I was inclined to laugh at the idea myself. In fact I even crossed him off our first list of suspects. But, there's every reason to believe he's our man. Except for hair colouring and eyes his description matches this man Kaffray. Contact lenses would alter his eyes and a simple dye job would fix his hair. The police are showing his photograph to Bradford Tower residents at this moment but I think the result is a foregone conclusion.' He stroked his chin thoughtfully. 'What I still can't figure out is where all this ties in with the Sphinx.'

Anne, who had been looking sadly at the accusing cover of Wilkinson's file, looked up sharply.

'The Sphinx? I don't understand.'

Her brother grinned ruefully.

'You and me both, Anne. It's part of some weird theory dreamed up by a Cambridge Professor.' Briefly he related Hughes's ideas to his sister.

Anne bit her lip slightly.

'So really what Griff and Hughes are suggesting is that Bill somehow sees himself as both protector and avenger of the innocents and at the same time is nursing a suicidal streak. In other words he knows that sooner or later somebody will catch up with him and he'll be killed. In order to help this along he's actually leaving a trail, like this Khafre - Kaffray business.'

Gerald nodded. 'That's how Griff sees it anyway.'

'But why would he do such a thing?'

Her brother shrugged with Latin theatricality. 'Who really knows, Anne? The shock of his family being wiped out so horribly unhinged him slightly. Or maybe he simply realises that the type of killing he's been doing can do funny things to a man's mind. Perhaps he just wants to be sure he's dead before he goes completely mad.'

Anne shivered.

'And if you catch him, is that what you'll do? Kill him?'

Parkinson didn't hesitate.

'No, not if we can help it, Anne. We don't go in for that sort of thing.'

Knowing her brother had never lied to her, but guessing he was probably doing so now, Anne nevertheless felt a slight sense of relief. Wondering why she did it she said slowly, 'Bill Wilkinson has an old tattoo of the Sphinx on his left wrist. It's very small. You'd hardly see it if he wore a watch. He - he said a lot of young soldiers had them done because it made them feel manly.'

Unbidden, two large tears formed in her wide green eyes and

rolled, like drops of crystal, down her smooth cheeks. With an odd gentleness Gerald laid his hand on her head.

'Do you know where he is, Anne?'

She sniffed, dabbed at her eyes with a tiny handkerchief, and smiled wanly.

'No, Gerry. He didn't turn up last night. I went round to that horrible place he lived in and the caretaker told me he hadn't been seen since Friday. I – I guess he's gone now for good?'

'Gerald, I think you had better come round to the office. I have a very large and extremely irate Scot here demanding to know what *you* have done with his daughter.' So spoke Sir Thomas Griff on the green telephone later that afternoon. As an afterthought the little man added, 'I think we owe him an explanation anyway.'

It was with some trepidation Gerald entered his chief's smoke-filled office some fifteen minutes later. In the time since he had joined Griff's rather peculiar organisation some seven years before Gerald Parkinson had met only two men he would not have cared to cross swords with. One was Griff's batman, cook, driver, companion and self-appointed bodyguard, ex-sergeant Donald Grace formerly of the Royal Air Force Regiment, who was, as far as Gerald knew, currently conducting Moira Fraser on a shopping expedition and doubtless enjoying every minute of it. Moira, now a guest in Griff's compact little establishment in Bayswater, had captivated the mighty sergeant from the moment she had set foot in the house. Even Griff had been driven to comment that not only was she allowed to beat the sergeant at crib but for the first time in living memory his grim, battered face appeared to wear a permanent smile. The second man, James Alistair Fraser, was, to Gerald's astonishment, comfortably established in Griff's office chatting amicably with the little man over a cup of coffee.

Griff looked up as Gerald walked into the office.

'Ah, Gerald,' he waved a small hand towards Fraser, looming large in a chair which seemed too small for his bulk, 'you know Mr Fraser, of course.'

Gerald nodded curtly to Fraser and received a grim-faced

acknowledgement. Lowering himself into a chair he crossed his legs and looked enquiringly at his chief. Griff cleared his throat a trifle theatrically.

'Now, Gerald, Mr Fraser here has very kindly cleared up a few points concerning his activities over the past two or three weeks and I am quite satisfied he could have had no part in the HAWL killings. Mr Fraser, in fact, has been negotiating the purchase of a substantial interest in an advertising agency which he intends to present to his daughter on the occasion of her twenty-third birthday in January of next year.' He grinned benignly. 'An occasion of which you are doubtless well aware, Gerald.'

Parkinson, who for two evenings on the trot had suddenly found occasion to visit the Griff home and had already arranged a third foray in order to pick up Miss Fraser and take her out to dine, had the grace to blush slightly. Fraser shot him a calculating look. Griff, a fresh cigar glowing well, carried on.

'I have taken the opportunity of acquainting Mr Fraser with some of the more salient facts concerning the HAWL affair. He has - er - some considerable experience in matters of this nature and I feel he may be able to assist our investigation in some way.'

Gerald shot his chief a surprised glance. This was not the little man's style at all. Normally he worked on the precept that the fewer people who knew what was going on the better. Much less chance of a leak. The little man's eyes beamed a silent warning. Parkinson relaxed. Griff continued.

'As I've said, Gerald, I've only given Mr Fraser the more general outline of what we think we are up against. Perhaps you, as the man closest to the action, might take it from here.'

Gerald, a separate section of his mind trying to work out what Griff might be up to, launched into a fairly comprehensive outline of the past few days events. As he repeated Professor Hughes's Sphinx theory something appeared to flicker behind Fraser's eyes. Gerald, his own eyes beginning to sting slightly from the smoke in the room, was not certain he had seen anything. When he glanced back at the big man, Fraser's hard face had closed up and his eyes reflected nothing more than casual interest. Presently, when Gerald had finished his recital, he stirred restlessly and spoke directly to Griff.

'So what is it you *really* want of me?'

Griff examined the tip of his cigar for a moment. When he looked up there was an odd glitter in his eyes.

'I think, Mr Fraser, you will agree that the burning of Fairlee Manor and its - er - contents will doubtless have broken the back of the Provisional IRA.'

Fraser grunted.

'Aye, I would say so. Nobody wants to die the way HAWL kills. What's left of that bunch will be too damned busy looking over their shoulders to worry about anything else. They won't be so damned worried about the supergrass system either because they would probably feel a hellova lot safer in prison. What will really worry them are the people they used to terrorise. They have found themselves a hero - someone who can give the Provos a taste of their own medicine - and sooner or later, those people are going to turn the bastards in or find a way of getting in touch with HAWL. Aye, they're finished all right - or at least for the time being.'

Griff nodded.

'My feelings exactly, Mr Fraser. Now, as a man who understands something of the professional soldier's outlook, what do you think HAWL would be likely to do next?'

Again Parkinson noticed something flare and die in the Scot's eyes. Jaf shrugged his massive shoulders.

'That's easy. He's put the fear of God into them now. Every terrorist who has heard of the killings will be wondering where he is likely to strike next. My bet is now he's got them pissing themselves he'll go after the big boys. The Russians, the Arabs, maybe even the Israelis or the Americans. None of them have clean hands. My money would be on the Russians or the Arabs.'

Griff added another stream of smoke to the fug in the room.

'Of the two, Mr Fraser, where do you think he will strike?'

Fraser's eyes were flat, almost hostile. 'You know the answer to that already.'

Griff waved his cigar gently. 'Perhaps, Mr Fraser,' he murmured. 'Perhaps I do. But I would like you to confirm.'

Fraser hesitated for a moment and his face tautened

suddenly. There was no mistaking his hostility now. It was patently obvious in his flat, malignant glare. Involuntarily Parkinson felt the fingers of his right hand flex slightly. But the hanging weight of the Colt under his arm seemed a great distance away from them. Jaf suddenly relaxed slightly.

'He killed an Arab didn't he? Quite probably tortured him first. I would say that's the way he would go.'

Griff nodded. His face displayed no awareness of the tension which had momentarily filled the room.

'Exactly what I was thinking.' He smiled suddenly and came round the desk holding out his hand. 'However, I think I have detained you both long enough. You will be anxious to see how well we have been looking after your daughter and I'm quite sure Gerald will be only too happy to run you round there.'

When the door had closed behind the two men Griff, cigar clamped between compressed lips, hands clasped behind his back, stood in the centre of the room and pensively studied the chair James Alistair Fraser had just vacated. Parkinson had been right in his assessment of the Scot. The man was undoubtedly dangerous but just how dangerous only time would tell.

Presently, having apparently made up his mind upon something, the little man returned to his desk and immediately buzzed for coffee. By the time his flustered secretary had brought it to him he was already engaged in the first of what were an apparently endless series of telephone calls.

Chapter Twenty

Mustapha Mirams was not a terrorist.

Neither, for that matter, was he involved in any way with terrorists, crooks, pimps, cheats or any other type of law-breaker. Mustapha was a Muslim, born in Notting Hill of immigrant parents and regarded by himself, and all who knew him, as a model, law-abiding, respectable Briton. His Pakistani parents had brought him up well and despite the many temptations about him Mustapha rigidly adhered to the tenets of Mohamed. It was this fact which saved his life.

Mustapha was a chauffeur. It was his job to groom, drive, and act as guardian to the big Mercedes 280 owned by his boss, Doctor Abdul Fulla. Mustapha had run the big Mercedes out into the dark mews behind the office block where it glittered wetly in the pouring rain. Knowing it would be a few minutes before he was called upon to take the car round to the front door Mustapha had produced his prayer mat and, at the back of the garage, was completing his final devotions of the day. Intent on his prayers Mustapha did not hear the light footfall behind him. Nor was he aware of the hand which sliced down on his exposed neck like a sword and sent him spinning into an endless black void.

Doctor Abdul Fulla was not a terrorist either. In fact it was doubtful if the Doctor had ever handled anything more lethal than a fountain pen in his life.

According to the shingle on the door of his impressive suite of offices Doctor Fulla was a practising psychiatrist. There were none who could testify to the Doctor's proficiency in his chosen field because remarkably few people ever attained the comfort of his inner office. His appointment book however was always impressively full which helped to discourage the odd off-the-cuff caller seeking his help.

Leila Angari, Doctor Fulla's beautiful, olive-skinned receptionist, *was* a terrorist.

Leila Angari was one of the many who claimed to be Palestinian and who had been born long after Palestine had vanished from the maps of the Western world. Leila had actually been born in a camp in Lebanon but she had, nevertheless, joined the PLO just before her thirteenth birthday. Almost a year later, before her fourteenth birthday, Leila was responsible for the placement of two bombs. The two bombs killed an Israeli mother and her two children and seven Arabs, one of them a woman. Leila never gave the Arabs a thought but was proud of the slaughter of the three Israelis. Possessed of a particularly virulent strain of blood lust and an inordinate sexual appetite she came quickly to the notice of her superiors and, following being bedded by a long-forgotten number of them, wound up in Libya for specialist training.

From there the young terrorist made several successful forays into the Western world and eventually was given the task she had held for four years. Not yet twenty-one, Leila was responsible for the safety of Doctor Abdul Fulla and for the screening of the few people who did eventually get to see him. In those four years she had been responsible for the abrupt demise of three people whom she had regarded as a threat to her charge.

Because Doctor Fulla was no ordinary man.

Abdul was Leila's lover and, despite his shy, rather retiring appearance, an extremely satisfying sexual athlete who could think of things to do with Leila not even *her* considerable experience could match. He was also, apart from his sexual prowess, the link man between various terrorist organisations and Gadaffi's money and arms.

Doctor Fulla and his striking receptionist were currently shrugging into their rainwear preparatory to leaving the office. Fulla had already buzzed the garage for the car but they would still have to make a run for it across the broad pavement. In this terrible weather they could hardly expect Mustapha to stand outside holding the car door open for them. Fulla was a very considerate employer and besides, both he and Leila were quite fond of the quiet, careful, unassuming chauffeur.

The big black Mercedes was waiting for them immediately opposite the door. Through the driving rain and the darkness they could just distinguish the vague outline of Mustapha's uniformed figure. He appeared to be adjusting the sliding glass hatch in the panel which Leila, for security reasons, had insisted be installed between driver and passengers. Hunching deeper into their raincoats the Doctor and Leila raced for the car through the pouring rain. Thankfully hurling themselves into the comfortable interior, Fulla pulled the door closed behind them.

Leila's sixth sense told her there was something wrong immediately. As the big car began to pull smoothly away from the kerb her eyes searched the interior while her fingers fumbled with the clasp of her handbag. When she saw it she knew it was already too late to try for the gun in her bag.

The can, enamelled a deep green, lay on the seat between her and the Doctor. It looked rather like a large can of gas lighter fuel except that the valve on this container was fully depressed. Leila had seen similar cans before. Knockout gas! Her arms suddenly seemed extraordinarily heavy but she struggled to reach for the door handle. It had gone and she knew the window button would be jammed. A moment before she slipped into unconsciousness Leila wondered remotely who was driving the car and what had happened to Mustapha.

It was just over half an hour before Mustapha Mirams regained consciousness. It took a minute or two for him to pull himself together and stagger to the telephone to call the police. It was two hours before a routine report on a possible kidnapping of two foreign nationals landed on the desk of an alert Special Branch officer. The Special Branch man, after ruminating for a minute or two, finally put his chances of promotion on the line and telephoned Sir Thomas Griff direct.

Griff listened attentively to all the officer had to say.

'Right. You say there's no reply from Fulla's office or his home, or, for that matter, from his receptionist's flat?'

'Correct, sir.'

'How long would you say since the chauffeur was knocked out?'

'Difficult to say, sir. The blow was intended to keep him out of circulation for some time. At a guess I would say around three hours.'

'And you say they were both Libyan nationals?'

'Yes, sir.'

Sir Thomas chewed the end of his cigar, something he detested watching other people doing.

'Right. Get into both the house and the office and see what you come up with. Don't waste any time. Break the doors down if you have to. Let me know immediately what you come up with.'

'But – but what about search warrants, sir?'

'Never mind the search warrants. Anybody questions you, tell them you have my full authority.'

'Right, sir. We'll get on it right away.'

The Special Branch officer closed the connection. He was halfway out of his office when it struck him he did not know whether Griff had the authority to issue such an order. In fact, all he knew about the man was confined to his telephone number and his name. He had no idea to what department or section the name belonged. He hesitated a moment and looked as if he might return to his desk. Then he shrugged. What the hell? He had his orders. He would worry about the authority later.

Gerald Parkinson and Moira Fraser were on the point of leaving Griff's Bayswater home for yet another evening out when the telephone sounded its urgent summons. Sergeant Grace, who had been engaged in a game of crib with Jaf, broke off the engagement to answer the call. Parkinson and Moira exchanged amused glances as the massive sergeant muttered into the instrument while keeping a watchful eye on Jaf in case he should be tempted to cheat.

Gerald, helping Moira into her wrap, grinned as he thought

of the initial meeting between the two huge men six days ago. It had made him think of two bull elephants warily circling each other in search of exploitable weaknesses. Jaf had the advantage of some two inches in height but the sergeant more than made up for that loss in the enormous width of his shoulders and massive depth of chest. Griff had been most insistent Moira and her father remain in the security of his care, and for the first two days the giants had hardly spoken more than a few reluctant grunts to each other. Moira, in the end, had brought them both to the crib board, a game they both loved, and since then the atmosphere had become a little more relaxed. The sergeant was now heard occasionally to refer to Jaf as 'sir' in deference to his rank.

Presently the sergeant's mutterings into the telephone ceased. He turned and held the instrument out to Parkinson.

'It's Sir Thomas, Mr Parkinson,' (no 'sir' for Gerald), 'he'd like to have a word with you if you don't mind.'

Grace's battered face implied that if Parkinson did mind, the instrument would immediately, and forcibly, be stuffed into a particularly tender part of his anatomy. Gerald accepted the proffered telephone.

'Parkinson here, sir.'

He listened for a time in silence. Presently his brow furrowed slightly but he said nothing. After a few more moments he said, 'OK, sir, I'll speak to him,' and replaced the receiver.

A crestfallen expression on his face, Gerald turned and spread his arms slightly in a gesture of resignation.

'I'm afraid our date's off, Moira. The old man thinks HAWL is at it again and wants me in the office straight away.' His eyes slid to Jaf's expressionless face. 'He'd like you to come along as well, Mr Fraser. If you don't mind.'

Jaf said nothing, but simply pushed back his chair and went to fetch his battered sheepskin.

Moira, some of the brightness gone from her eyes, looked for some form of reassurance in Grace's battered features. The gargoyle-like face creased into a grin and a huge paw rested on her slim shoulder for a moment.

'Don't you fret, Miss Moira. Nothing's going to happen to young Mr Parkinson here while your Dad's around.'

It was the closest Grace was ever to come to admitting he might conceivably have met his match in James Alistair Fraser.

Griff's office was, as might be expected, swimming in tobacco smoke when Jaf and Parkinson entered. The little man, a fresh Napoleon going full blast, looked up from what appeared to be several sheets of computer printouts and waved the two men into chairs.

'A little over five hours ago,' he began without preamble, 'a Libyan doctor and his receptionist were apparently abducted. Special Branch now inform me that the receptionist is a known PLO terrorist who apparently has worked out of Libya for some years.' He paused a moment as if gathering his thoughts. 'What is more interesting, however, is that the doctor, although himself not an active terrorist, appears to have been the link man between several European terrorist groups and Gaddafi. The fool was stupid enough to keep records of his various transactions at his home – presumably for the purpose of eventually letting his boss see how honest he'd been.

'Special Branch, of course, are now behaving like a dog with two tails and are in the process of rounding up those listed in Fulla's records before they learn of what has happened. However, there is obviously a strong possibility that HAWL has these people. Their abduction could, of course, be the work of some disgruntled group Fulla has dealt with in the past but I am inclined to discard that possibility.'

The smoke around his desk thickened visibly.

'Now I'm sure I need not tell you that what a mine of information those two could prove to be to HAWL, nor, for that matter the use to which HAWL will undoubtedly put that information. The thing is, gentlemen, HAWL has only a few hours' start on us. We have to find him, either before he gets that information or before he can use it.'

Parkinson could scarcely bring himself to believe his ears. Here was the head of perhaps the most secret security organisation in the world blithely discussing a project with a virtually unknown outsider. Obviously it was being done for some purpose but even taking Griff's convoluted thinking into consideration he could find no valid reason for Fraser's presence at this meeting. The man's undoubted hostility to what they were trying to do had been amply demonstrated on the last occasion they had talked in this office. Whatever Griff might be up to, it made no sense to Gerald. He held his peace however, and stuck to the immediate problem.

'That's fine as far as it goes, sir. But we have to find HAWL before we can do anything about stopping him.'

Griff's eyes glittered through the smoke.

'Quite correct, Gerald. But, as you know, we have been doing some work on that score.'

Gerald nodded.

'You mean the banks, sir?'

'Precisely.' The little man tapped the printouts on his desk. 'Now, taking our friend Professor Hughes's theory on the Sphinx into consideration I decided to test it as regards its practicality.

'Our first step was to find out where our vanished Mr Kaffray kept his money. That was relatively simple because he paid his lease at the Bradford by cheque. Having got that far we then investigated his account. Using Hughes's theory I was looking for several key names; they were Thebes, Giza, Oedipus and Sphinx. Kaffray we already knew about.

'We found that in the course of his alleged business dealings several large sums passed between Mr Kaffray's account and that of a small trading company called Thebes International run, apparently, by a gentleman with the name Georges P. Eedipous. A run down on the Thebes account then uncovered considerable dealings with Giza Enterprises, run by a Mr Terence Giza.

'The pattern, of course, was then fairly obvious. The money originally obtained from the robberies was fed into these accounts and simply kept on the move.' He paused and looked at the two men. 'Are you with me so far?'

Gerald nodded and shot a surreptitious glance at Fraser. The big man had his gaze firmly fixed on Griff's mobile features. There was an odd raptness on the big man's hard face which the younger man found strangely disturbing. Griff continued.

'The next step, of course, was to discover where these

gentlemen lived – or were supposed to live. That took a little more time. However, taking the easiest route and assuming that the residences would at least be close to the business addresses – one was in Wiltshire and the other in Hertfordshire – we searched the voters' lists and contacted every estate agent in both counties. Quite a considerable operation, I can assure you. Eventually we came up trumps. Both men have apparently purchased country residences this year.

'Now Mr Georges P. Eedipous has a country house a few miles from Stevenage. My bet is that because it is closer to the city this is where HAWL will take his prisoners. Also, it would appear to be the next step in the pattern. Oedipus going to Thebes.'

The little man rummaged among the papers on his desk, found what he was looking for, and handed a slip of paper to Gerald.

'Those are the addresses. Now don't waste time. I want you up in Stevenage as fast as you can. We may just get lucky. I suggest you go downstairs with Mr Fraser and draw arms for each of you.' His piercing eyes focussed on the big Scot for a moment. 'I take it, Mr Fraser, you have no objections to accompanying Gerald? Your – er – knowledge will doubtless be of considerable use to him.'

For a moment the big man looked as if he might object. He cleared his throat as if to say something then changed his mind and simply shook his head.

'Good, good,' Griff said happily. He waved his cigar in a slightly imperious gesture of dismissal. 'Off you go then,' he said, as though he was talking to a party of schoolchildren going off on a picnic. 'Just remember we may have him cornered this time, so do try and be careful.'

Ten minutes after a bemused Parkinson and a grimly silent Fraser had left his smoke-filled office, Sir Thomas picked up the telephone and quickly dialled a local number. His conversation, when he received acknowledgement, was brief to the extreme.

'They've gone,' he said quietly. 'Stand by.'

Chapter Twenty-One

A great sense of extreme tiredness enveloped him. His shoulders sagged, his arms and legs were strangely heavy and unwieldy as he moved around the tiny, low ceilinged living room. His stomach heaved. He felt a brackish rush of bile to the back of his throat. Gagging slightly, he hoped he was not going to be sick again. There couldn't be damned much left in his stomach to throw up.

Wearily he stripped off his blood-soaked coveralls and allowed them to drop in an ugly heap on the carpet. What he needed was a shower and several hours of sleep. Perhaps if he took an extra Valium it would knock him out completely and keep the nightmares away. It seemed there was no way he could lose the echoing screams in his head no matter what he tried.

He put the comforting thought of sleep from his head. He would not have time for that. Somewhere, somebody was beginning to put two and two together. When they finally got the sum completed it would not take too long for them to find him.

Naked, he padded tiredly to the shower. Stepping under it he allowed the needle spray to lance over him. The water swirling around his feet assumed a faintly pinkish tinge then gradually cleared.

This time, at least, it had been mercifully quick.

The woman, however, for all her supposed toughness, had been a problem. By the time he had finished working on Fulla – and *he* had talked at the first bite of the hacksaw – she had been literally gibbering with fear. Almost ceaselessly she had babbled and shrieked and begged for mercy. Urine streaming down her naked thighs she had promised him willing compliance to every vile deviation she could think of if he would only spare her. In the end it had proved too much for him and he had simply broken her neck. What he had done to the man would be enough.

He wondered vaguely if it had all been worth it. Would things, in the end, really work out as he had planned them? He pushed that thought from his mind also. It was useless to wonder about it. It was something he would never know. Meanwhile he had to get dressed, make his telephone call, and go.

Tim Carter, unusually, had not yet left the *Express* building. He was trying, on his editor's instructions, to put together a piece on the HAWL killings for the Sunday edition. So far he had made quite a number of false starts and his crammed wastepaper basket bore mute testimony to his abortive labours. Tim was having trouble following the *Express* line that HAWL, despite its methods, was doing a much needed job. The memory of the grisly remains on the lawn of Fairlee Manor was still too fresh in his mind to allow him to be even remotely objective.

Strangely the hacked-about corpses at Roseford Farm had not affected him quite so badly. Somehow a piece of his mind could understand and, to a degree, accept the mutilation. But to cold-bloodedly turn fire on a fellow human was another matter. What kind of people could do such a thing? What sick mind could conceive and execute such a plan? True, the dead men had been terrorists, murderers of the worst kind, but had they really deserved to die in such a horrible and grotesque manner?

His grizzled editor, appreciating his young reporter's problem, had no doubt whatsoever. Calling Tim into his office, he closed the door for a few minutes.

'Tim, laddie, I think you're going to have to make your mind up once and for all whether you're on the side of the goodies or the baddies.

'Now, you have a bonnie wee wife who thinks the sun rises and sets on your bum. At the moment her main worries are whether you'll be able to afford a microwave cooker if the Government hammers you for more income tax, or whether you can afford a baby yet. What if she suddenly had to worry about bombs going off in the local supermarket?

'How, my lad, would *you* feel, if while she's out trying to find you a nice steak for your supper, a bomb goes off and she loses an arm, or a leg, or, worse still, is killed? What do you think would go on in your head if some nutcase calmly announced that the bomb had been planted to draw attention to the movement for the Independence of Canvey Island?

'You have to realise that it's people like your wee wife the terrorists are really aiming at. If they can put the fear of God into people like her then sooner or later she is going to get herself a weapon of some kind or scream at the Government to put soldiers in the street and arm the police. When that happens then little by little the fabric of law and order begins to tear itself apart.

'Do ye not understand, laddie? Bombs are blind things. They don't know who they're killing and the people who plant the bombs know that. But they don't give a damn. They're not in the least interested in *who* they kill. The purpose is to instil terror, and to hell with who suffers.

'Well, HAWL understands all this too. But there's no indiscriminate bombing with them. They use terror differently. They direct it straight at the terrorist by using the most horrible methods they can think of. I'll bet there isn't a man alive who thinks Canvey Island's Independence is worth being incinerated or having his balls dangling in front of his eyes. Not, of course, that terrorist movements don't like martyrs. They love them – just so long as the martyr is somebody else. But being a martyr is one thing and being a chunk of mince is another.

'Now, laddie, thanks to HAWL it's the terrorists who are shitting themselves. Not you, not me, not that bonnie wee wife of yours, but the same indiscriminate killers who suddenly find it's not so funny on the other side of the fence.

'Long may HAWL keep up the good work, I say. Now away

you go and write that piece and shed no tears over dead terrorists.'

His editor's lecture notwithstanding Tim still could not settle himself to write the piece. He had just ripped his umpteenth attempt from his typewriter when his telephone rang.

The last voice in the world that Tim Carter wanted to hear at that moment sounded flatly in his ear.

Five minutes later, Tim, his stomach behaving oddly (because apparently there was a woman involved this time), was speaking to Sir Thomas Griff. Sir Thomas, as usual, heard him through in silence. Tim could imagine the little man calmly sucking at his cigar or perhaps taking an occasional sip at a fresh cup of coffee. Griff's voice, when he finally spoke, was unusually crisp.

'You're quite sure he said Hertfordshire, Tim?'

'Yes, sir. Blackstone Cottage, Stevenage, Hertfordshire.'

'Thank you, Tim. Goodnight.'

'Er – goodnight, sir.'

Griff, for once without a Napoleon burning, sat for some time following Tim Carter's call staring blankly at a spot just above the door. After a time, his mind still obviously engaged with something only he could see, he groped blindly for the ever present box and selected a cigar. For a moment or two his attention was taken up with the mechanics of stripping the wrapper and ascertaining the weed burned evenly. Then, with satisfactory dragons of smoke writhing towards the ceiling, he learned forward and pulled the telephone towards him.

For a moment he hesitated.

Whatever caused his slight delay vanished abruptly. Glancing at his watch, he lifted the receiver and dialled a number. Someone at the other end had obviously been awaiting the call. The receiver was lifted before the first ring had been completed.

'You have a few hours,' Griff said quietly. 'No, I can't tell you exactly. I would guess at around six at the outside.' He listened a moment more then said, 'goodbye,' and replaced the instrument on its cradle.

Puffing strongly at his cigar the little man glanced at his watch once more. Eleven forty-five. It was going to be a long night.

Approximately fifteen minutes after Sir Thomas Griff had made his telephone call, three large cars filed out from an underground car park near Hyde Park and nosed into the quietening traffic. After sifting through a maze of one-way streets, the little convoy settled down to cruise out of the city in a westerly direction.

Each of the three cars contained four men and a driver. There was little or no conversation in any of the vehicles. Each man appeared wholly occupied with his own thoughts and simply gazed blankly through his window at the wet, gleaming streets as they slid by. If there was anything at all to raise comment about the silent convoy it would be the rather odd fact that every man wore a dark suit and shirt. To the odd casual observer it might appear that each vehicle was occupied only by disembodied heads.

Chapter Twenty-Two

For some time after they had left Griff's office Parkinson and Fraser travelled in silence. Gerald, as he swung the big Jaguar through wet and dismal streets, was still trying to make sense of Griff's uncharacteristic moves.

Why, for example, had the big, grim-faced man sitting alongside him been made privy to what they were doing to counter HAWL? Fraser was undoubtedly dangerous and there was no denying in which direction his sympathies lay. Not, of course, that Gerald could blame him for that. The man's wife had been killed by a terrorist bomb. The same bomb, in fact, which had wiped out Wilkinson's family.

Was there, he thought angrily, a link between Fraser and Wilkinson? Could he, perhaps, be travelling with a HAWL ally, prepared to hinder rather than assist the project? The thought was far from pleasant. Gerald comforted himself with the thought that the same notion must have occurred to Griff. The little man would hardly have issued the man with a highly illegal weapon had he thought there was any danger of it being turned against one of his own agents.

His thoughts now channelled back to their starting point, Gerald again tried to figure out just what the little man was up to. He knew, from past experience, that there was a great deal more to the little man than met the eye, but this time there was no way Parkinson could follow his thinking. There were far too many anomalies about this project. Why, for example, had Griff not sent for those dossiers earlier? He must have known that they would exist for at least three of their suspects. And why, for that matter, had Griff so suddenly changed his mind from thinking that HAWL was an organisation to it being a solitary man?

Gerald was convinced there was some sort of pattern to what was going on but he could not quite put his finger on it. Somewhere there was a reason for it all – a very definite purpose. But strive as he might he could not find the key to Griff's strategy.

His over-active mind returned to Jaf. The mercenary troubled him a great deal more than he cared to admit. What, he wondered for the umpteenth time, was he doing here?

'You appear to be seeing a lot of my daughter, Parkinson.'

Jaf's low growl shattered Gerald's thoughts and brought him back to the immediate present. He had been seeing a lot of Moira and fully intended seeing a great deal more of her in future because, to his great astonishment, Parkinson had fallen in love. What, as far as Gerald was concerned, was a great deal more important was that he was certain his feelings were reciprocated. He hoped Fraser was not about to play the heavy father. It was quite bad enough knowing the man was a killer without having to contemplate him as a father-in-law.

'Er – yes, Jaf. As a matter of fact I have,' he said quietly. 'I happen to think she's a very fine girl.'

Gerald's fears about the heavy-handed father were dispelled by Jaf's next comment.

'Good, good. It's about time she started getting a bit of fun out of life. Since her mother died she seems to have got the idea that her mission is to look after me.' He let out a low, rumbling sound which Gerald was astonished to recognise as a chuckle. 'Dammit, I'm hardly the type to need mothering.'

In spite of himself, Gerald found himself grinning at the thought of this enormous, self-sufficient man being mothered by anyone. Jaf must have caught the glitter of his teeth.

'Aye, well might you smile. But nevertheless that's what she's been trying to do and it's worried the hell out of me. I mean in my kind of work I'm not always going to be around, am I?' A huge hand reached out of nowhere and rested a moment on Gerald's shoulder. 'Just go easy. I wouldn't like to see her hurt.'

* * *

The Mercedes cruised effortlessly in a south-westerly direction and, with the roads comparatively clear, he had ample time to think of his next move. There was little doubt it was going to be a difficult one. Now that he had the information he required it was going to be one hell of a job to put it to good use.

Fixing his eyes on the ribbon of road winding before his headlights, he concentrated a part of his mind on the problem.

Getting into the damned place was the secret. Getting out didn't matter. Could it be done with a fast vehicle? He discarded that thought almost immediately. No point in getting himself killed *before* he got to them, and there was virtually no chance of a vehicle making it past the gate no matter how fast it was moving. A sharp lesson had been learned from the Iranian-inspired bombing of the French and American army headquarters in Beirut. Those had been done by vehicles loaded with high explosives and driven through the gates at high speed by suicidal zealots. They'd simply shoot out the tyres of anything moving above walking pace and he wouldn't have a hope in hell on foot. The place was only vulnerable from above and how could a hostile aircraft even get close?

The lights of an all-night filling station and café gleaming ahead made him suddenly conscious of his empty stomach. The savage churning had gone now as it usually did after an hour or two. He thought maybe he could eat something and keep it down. Flicking his indicator switch, he pulled into the slow lane. As he pulled off the motorway and slid the car into an empty parking slot the solution struck him. He sat a moment behind the wheel.

A chopper!

Given a mercenary pilot who wouldn't ask questions provided the money was right, and he would be among them before they knew what was hitting them. Simple really. Give the chopper a new coat of paint, change the insignia, and they might even welcome him with open arms. Opening the door, he swung his legs out into the cold night air. The chopper was definitely the answer. He would settle down to working out the details later.

Stretching himself, he paused a moment as, for some reason, a sense of stillness descended upon him. For a fleeting second it appeared as if the entire world had come to a standstill and he was aware of an inner feeling of absolute peace and calm. He had known that feeling before. As suddenly as it had come it was gone and he became aware of noise and motion once more.

Shrugging slightly as if from the impact of the raw, cold air, he reached back into the car. Opening the glove compartment he extracted a small stamped and addressed packet. He locked the car door carefully and made his way briskly towards the warm lights of the café. Perhaps he had better not lay too many plans just yet.

There was a post box set in the wall of the café foyer. Glancing down at the address on the packet he walked over to it. His lips twitched slightly and his eyes softened with a gentle sadness. Then he dropped the packet into the yawning maw of the post box and it was gone. It was addressed to Anne Parkinson.

Sir Thomas Griff lit yet another Napoleon and for the hundredth time glanced at his watch.

One thirty-five.

Leaning forward, he depressed a button on his intercom. His secretary answered him immediately.

'Yes, Sir Thomas?'

Griff cleared his throat.

'Miss Alexander, for the next few hours I am not to be disturbed unless it's by the P.M. himself. I want only the green line open.'

'Yes, sir. And it's Miss Ringold, sir.'

Much to Gerald's surprise, Fraser, on the run northwards, had proved surprisingly loquacious and had regaled the younger man with a series of anecdotes concerning the big man's exploits as a mercenary in various countries. Parkinson had been more than a little surprised to learn that twice during his colourful career the Scot had been employed by the British. For what purpose, or to which country however, the mercenary chose not to disclose. Gerald also noticed that Fraser's stories mostly related to the funnier side of his exploits and practically nothing of the hairier part of his calling.

All in all, as they began to approach Stevenage and cast about for Blackstone Cottage, Gerald found himself warming slightly to the big mercenary. Like Griff, there appeared to be a great deal more to the Scot than met the eye. Nevertheless at the back of his mind he was still wary of the man. He killed too easily. A fact which Gerald had good cause to remember and which had been made more apparent by Jaf's selection of a hand-gun from the wide range held in the basement armoury.

Gerald had, as usual, selected his favourite, the cylinder action Colt Special. The big man mocked his choice.

'You're not going to do much damage with that thing, Parkinson,' he grunted. 'If you're going to carry a gun at all then at least make it one which makes the effort worthwhile. With that Colt you're going to have to walk up and stick it in the other fellow's ear before you can do any good with it.'

Gerald flushed angrily. He liked the Colt and considered himself extremely proficient with it.

'Yes, but at least with this I have less chance of a jam at the wrong time.'

'Aye,' the Scot agreed, 'but its effective range is minimal and it takes a wee bit of time to reload. The other fellow isn't going to sit on his arse and wait for you to stuff shells into those chambers, and remember, he's going to have the advantage of at least eight shots to your six, plus the fact that he can change magazines in double quick time.' He held up the gun he had been examining, a Czech M52 similar to the one he had used so effectively at Sedgefield. 'Now *this* is a different kettle of fish. Fires a 7.62 cartridge and has a muzzle velocity of 1600 feet per second. Has an eight round magazine, can fire up to thirty rounds per minute, and has an effective range of seventy yards. That, my friend, is about half as far again as most hand-guns and probably twice the range of that pop-gun of yours. Now with a cartridge as powerful as these buggers if I hit somebody then he's going to stay hit because it will feel like a bus struck him.' He grinned wolfishly. 'When you carry a gun, laddie, it's not for the fun of it.'

Now, pulling into an all-night filling station to fuel up and enquire as to the whereabouts of Blackstone Cottage, Gerald found himself wondering again at Griff's turning this man loose with a gun.

Blackstone, they discovered, was a small development of modern villas some two miles back the way they had come. Blackstone Cottage, from where the new development apparently had gained its name, was a converted blacksmith's shop some half mile or so from the cluster of modern buildings.

The long, low, thatch-roofed structure had an oddly deserted look about it as they cautiously surveyed its outlines from a distance of about forty feet. The rain had stopped but the sullen night sky was heavily overhung with cloud. What little moonlight there was illumined the whitewashed walls only pallidly but sufficient for them to determine nothing appeared to be moving. No lights showed. The small windows glowered blindly back at them.

Gerald felt instinctively that the man they wanted had gone. There was nothing alive in the building.

'I think he's gone,' he whispered hoarsely.

'Aye, I think you're right,' agreed the Scot. 'But you hang on there while I take a look. If anything goes wrong see what you can do to help with that water pistol of yours.'

Suiting his actions to his words, the big man moved noiselessly away and, to all intents and purposes, vanished. Marvelling yet again at the big man's uncanny ability to move invisibly and silently Gerald strained his eyes towards the cottage. If this turned out to be some kind of trap he'd have to be prepared to rush to the Scot's aid. The damp, raw air was beginning to seep into his bones when the cottage lights were switched on. Fraser's huge frame was suddenly silhouetted in the doorway. The big man waved him in.

A few minutes later, Gerald, ashen-faced, spoke to Sir Thomas on the green line.

'Well, Gerald?'

'He's gone, sir.'

'Hmmm. I was afraid of that. And the Libyans?'

'Dead, sir. We found them in the garage. The man's in a mess – place is covered in blood – but he left the woman alone. Broke her neck.'

'Any idea how long he's been gone?'

'Not for certain, sir. But Fraser thinks he's maybe got a three hour start on us.'

There was a moment's silence from the other end of the line then Gerald distinctly heard the rasp of a match. God, he thought, the cold-blooded little bastard's lighting a cigar while he thinks out his next move. He wondered for a moment at his flash of anger before Griff spoke again.

'Gerald?'

'Yes, sir.'

'Unless he has a bolthole, which doesn't figure in the Sphinx theory, he'll be heading for Wiltshire. You better get moving down there.'

'Yes, sir.'

'And, Gerald' – a slight pause – 'Get out of that house. The police will be on their way and we don't need any awkward questions.'

Chapter Twenty-Three

They had been back on the road just over half an hour when the thought struck Gerald. It came straight out of the blue and it hit him hard. So hard, in fact, that he unconsciously eased back his foot on the accelerator and the powerful car slowed perceptibly.

How could Griff possibly have known the police were on their way to Blackstone cottage?

Following hard on the heels of the question came the answer: the *Express* and Tim Carter. Following his usual procedure HAWL would have telephoned Carter at the *Express* and Tim would have followed through with his usual alerts to Griff and Special Branch.

Griff had made it a standing rule that on the HAWL project he wanted hourly reports. Yet when Gerald had telephoned his last report Griff had not mentioned any call from the *Express.* And, when he had made the call from the cottage, the little man had actually enquired after the Libyans and again had made no mention of the fact he already knew they were dead.

Why?

The car slowed to a virtual crawl. Jaf shot a sharp glance at his companion.

'What's up?' he growled. 'Something wrong with the car?'

Fraser's question snapped Gerald from his shocked reverie. Shaking his head slightly he put his foot down once more. The powerful engine responded with a muted roar and the big Jaguar leaped forward.

'No, nothing wrong with the car, Jaf. I was just trying to figure out what Griff is up to.'

Fraser laughed harshly.

'I thought you were a little more intelligent, Gerry.' Parkinson blinked at this familiar use of his name but said nothing as the big man continued. 'Griff simply wants HAWL dead. The man has taken the guts out of the Provisional IRA but now that he appears to have shifted his attention to other terrorist organisations he will become a major embarrassment. Britain can't afford that.'

Several things suddenly fell into place. Griff had known about Wilkinson's past right from the beginning and, since the man appeared to be waging a winning battle with the IRA, the little man had said nothing. The sudden switch to the single man theory had come only after HAWL had wiped out half the Provo leadership. Griff had deliberately fostered the group idea until such time as the Provos had been terrorised into manageable levels. He had known the Libyans were dead some time before Gerald had reported but had deliberately withheld the information.

Why?

To keep him off the trail and slow him down.

Gerald felt suddenly angry and at the same time was conscious of a vague sense of betrayal. There could only be one possible reason why Griff had deliberately slowed him down. Because he needed more time. The little man had set up another operation to wipe out HAWL. Probably with the Arabs or the Russians or maybe even the CIA. That way *his* hands would be clean. Nobody would be able to point a finger at the British as having wiped out the terrorist exterminator whom a large percentage of the public at large now regarded as something of a hero.

'And what, exactly, is your place in all this, Jaf?' Gerald asked bitterly. 'I suppose you've been sent along to make sure Wilkinson dies.'

Jaf's voice was suddenly angry.

'Don't talk like a bloody idiot. If anybody should be inclined to Wilkinson's side it would be me. Don't you think your boss knows that? After all, I'm hardly going to kill the man who's been doing such a damned good job of wiping out the people who were responsible for my wife's death. I don't know any more than you do about why I'm here but at least I can make an intelligent guess.'

Parkinson swallowed his anger and swung the powerful car out to overtake a large truck trundling along in the wrong lane.

'All right,' he gritted. 'Suppose you tell me why you think you're here.'

Fraser's face cracked in a mirthless grin.

'It's just as I tried to tell you back at the armoury. When you carry a gun it's not because you need the ballast. You have to be prepared to use it in the most effective manner possible. Your problem is that you are still wet behind the ears when it comes down to the really rough stuff. You may even have used that gun of yours once or twice but you regard it more as a toy or a badge of office than anything else.

'You're not playing cowboys and Indians you know. It's not just a question of saying "bang, you're dead", and then getting back up and having another go. When you go "bang" in real life you have to be damned certain the other man doesn't get up to have another go.'

Gerald momentarily took his eyes from the road and glared angrily at the man in the seat beside him. Jaf held up a huge hand.

'There's no point in getting yourself annoyed, laddie. This isn't between the good guys and the bad guys. It makes no difference which side you're on. It's a question of living or dying. Right now we're heading towards some people who know the rules a damned sight better than you do. Wilkinson, if you remember, is one of the most highly trained fighting men in the world. The people who are after him will know that, so they won't be putting incompetents in the field either. What, my lad, we are heading into is a small war with no questions being asked by either side. Believe me, there will be no room for neutrals.'

The big man's hard face tautened.

'I think Griff is aware you may have shortcomings in a situation like this. I believe, rightly or wrongly, I'm here to see you come out alive - providing, of course, Wilkinson isn't already dead.'

* * *

He was in no particular hurry.

A light meal of scrambled eggs and toast had made him feel slightly better and, to his relief, he had managed to keep it down. Enjoying the warmth and return to normality caused by the presence of a few late travellers he had lingered over several cups of coffee for more than an hour. Now he was back on the road gently easing the purring Mercedes towards his final refuge in England.

He was fond of Abbey House. It was the kind of place Caroline and Jennifer would have loved had they ever been able to afford it. Even its name implied a certain sense of tranquility and peace.

It had been built just before the Second World War as a country residence for a wealthy clothing manufacturer with an eye for the natural beauty of the Downs. A pleasant, red brick, two storey structure it nestled comfortably in a tree-filled fold in the rolling countryside and proudly stood watch over the six acres of parkland comprising its grounds. A small stream, crystal clear in summer but swollen and brown now with the winter rains, meandered through the exact centre of the small estate and was crossed by a picturesque wooden footbridge. It was, in summer, with the chestnuts and sycamores in full leaf, a spot of particular beauty which could never fail to stir the heart of the beholder. Even now, with the glorious shades of autumn long gone and the trees starkly naked it was still a pleasant, peaceful spot.

There were those who said it was an isolated, lonely place. But its solitary calm suited him. Occasionally, when he was there, wandering through the grounds, he would half regret the course he had chosen for himself.

Cruising past a signpost he noted that Stonehenge was only fifteen miles away. He brightened. A little of his tiredness fell away. It wouldn't be long now.

Gerald, not quite certain why he should be rushing to the aid of a killer, sent the big Jaguar hurtling out of Berkshire into Wiltshire. Somewhere on this dark, rushing drive his attitude towards HAWL had undergone a radical change and he could not understand it. He put it down to the fact that he did not like the idea of any man being shot down like a dog but at the back of his mind he knew it was something more. He did not dare probe his motives too deeply.

'We're in the top end of Wiltshire now, Jaf,' he said quietly, keeping his eyes fixed on the road. 'There's a survey map in the glove pocket. Better start looking for Abbey House. The map has an inch to the mile scale so it should show up all right.'

Jaf grunted and, leaning forward, rummaged in the glove pocket. Presently, with the aid of a small hand torch, he began studying the map. He located Abbey House in a few minutes.

'OK, I've got it. It's quite a way off yet. Keep going as you are until I tell you to turn off. After that, when I tell you to slow down, do just that.'

Parkinson gritted his teeth. There were times when Jaf made him feel positively murderous.

'Why slow down?' he snapped. 'I thought we were in a hurry?'

'Damn it,' snarled Jaf. 'Just do as you're bloody well told, will you? It's four forty-five in the morning and sound travels a long way at this time. You don't want to warn everybody in the neighbourhood we're coming, do you?'

Gerald clamped his mouth shut and concentrated on his driving.

Sir Thomas Griff stepped rather stiffly from behind his desk and, small hands clasped behind his back, began to pace sedately around his office. The little man was becoming concerned. For some reason the hourly calls from Parkinson had ceased. So far he had missed two deadlines and, by the look of things, was about to miss another. Griff did not like it. Something was wrong. Things were not going quite according to plan.

He glanced at his watch. Five-o-five. Surely he would hear something soon.

Abbot's Hill formed the west flank of the fold in which lay Abbey House.

Where the names had originally come from he had no idea

but presumed that there had once been an Abbey somewhere in the area. But he was not interested in the source of the names as he pulled the Mercedes off the road just round the bend from the northern flank of the gentle, tree-dotted slope. Abbot's Hill had the advantage of being the highest point above the house and from it he could look directly down into his property. It had been his habit since buying the place to recce the area from this point before taking the winding road into it. The corkscrew road was just too handy for an ambush.

Killing the sidelights he had been driving on for the past mile, he eased himself out of the car and quietly snicked the door shut. Soundlessly he moved to the boot and lifted the hood. Swiftly he uncovered his gun belt from the folds of a black rollneck sweater. His movements precise, he stripped off his sports jacket and shrugged into the sweater. Buckling the belt round his waist he tested the buckle and, ears cocked for the slightest sound, performed his twisting ritual. Sometimes he smiled as he carried out these precautions. This morning, as he softly closed the boot, there was no flicker of humour on his grim face.

Chapter Twenty-Four

Why he did it Bill Wilkinson never knew.

Perhaps it was instinct or simply a soldier's intuitive feeling that all was not well, but whatever it was it took him down the slope of Abbot's Hill and brought him, in the end, face to face with the enemy and his destiny.

For some few minutes he stood on the silent hill scanning the house and grounds through a powerful pair of night glasses designed to pick up and amplify what little light was available. Nothing moved. Not even a shadow flickered, yet something was niggling at him like the dull throb of an aching tooth. He half thought of returning to the Mercedes and getting out fast but he rejected the idea. He decided, in the end, to go down on foot and scout the area. Totally confident in his own ability to avoid detection, he had no sooner made the decision than he was on the move flitting from tree to shadow like a ghost.

His progress, however, did not go undetected.

Sergei Petrovitch, scanning the entire area through an infra-red heat scope, missed his advent on his first pass over the hill area but his return sweep picked up the hazy flicker of his body heat. Sergei concentrated his attention on the moving swirl in his scope. Either a large animal was coming down through the trees or their man had chosen to try and come in through the back door. He fiddled with the image intensifier but saw no movement. He had heard the Americans had much better scopes and he wished fervently he had one now.

Hastily he moved the awkward, bulbous scope lower. Almost immediately he picked up what he was seeking. His two men were still in position. If that was HAWL coming down the hill then in a few moments he was going to run smack into two very tough men indeed. He would die before he was even aware of their existence. He took the scope from his eyes and stared across at the hill bulking black against the sky. He could see nothing and was forced to resort to the scope once more. Almost immediately he picked them up. The crazy, red, wavering patterns were almost one. They were virtually on top of each other. Convinced he had spotted the arrival of HAWL and was probably about to witness his demise, he kept his eyes glued to the awkward scope.

But Sergei Petrovitch had not taken several things into account.

Wilkinson, moving noiselessly and with remarkable speed was coming downhill and both Russians were facing into the Estate. Three things struck Wilkinson simultaneously. He realised what had struck him as wrong: there was a complete absence of night sound, no scufflings, rustlings, or sleepy chirpings or squeaks, as if the tiny creatures of the night were aware there was danger about; and, almost immediately, he caught the faint odour of tobacco as it clung to someone's clothing plus the faint, sickly smell of sweat.

Wilkinson froze. He was not alone and whoever lay in wait for him was not very far away - in fact, he had to be almost on top of him. His eyes probed the darkness searching for deeper shadows, more solid shapes.

Slightly to the right of where he was standing, Wilkinson could vaguely discern the outline of a large granite rock which jutted like a wart from the green slope of the hill. As he studied it, the outline of the rock appeared to alter slightly. His eyes, drawn by this phenomenon, focussed sharply on the dark bulk. Gradually he became aware of deeper, more inconsistent shadows: two men, less than ten feet away, mercifully facing down towards the house.

His heart kicked violently and he was aware of a momentary feeling of exhilaration as adrenalin pumped massively through his system. His hand swept down and up and, even as the knife left it, his powerful legs gathered beneath him and he hurled himself out and down towards the second of the two men. He heard the blade thud home and the startled, gasping grunt of its victim just before his feet smashed into the second watcher, driving his face savagely against the granite.

With the agility of a cat Wilkinson used the leverage of the impact to twist himself back and land on his feet. There was time to find out what damage he had done. He had to be certain. The second of his two knives leaped into his right hand, his left seized a handful of greasy hair and wrenched the head back on a thick neck. The razor-sharp blade swept swiftly across the exposed throat.

The first man, Wilkinson's knife buried in his back, turned, gurgling softly and in a sudden burst of energy tried to bring a Kalashnikov to bear on the swiftly moving shadow. Wilkinson's second blade thudded up under his ribcage before the barrel reached waist height.

Stooping to retrieve his knives Wilkinson was startled by the staccato chatter of automatic gunfire from the direction of the road.

'Stop the car!'

Obedient to Jaf's terse command, Gerald slammed his foot on the brake. Turning his head he found the Scot casually testing the mechanism of the M52. Jaf's teeth glittered briefly.

'About a quarter mile further on there's a road cuts off to your right. Just over a mile along that road, also on your right, is the entrance to Abbey House. As soon as you turn off this road I want you to douse the headlights and we'll travel the rest on sidelights only or, better still, no lights at all if you can manage it. But – ' his teeth shone again, 'I want you to keep your hand on the headlight switch and when I give you the nod I want the headlights switched on fast. Now have you got that?'

Gerald, his mouth suddenly dry, nodded his head.

Jaf laughed harshly, a sound which gave Gerald no comfort whatsoever.

'Better keep that popgun of yours handy as well. Maybe we'll get a chance to see how good you are with it. Now, let's go.'

The narrow country road was lined either side by tall hedgerows and twisted so tortuously that even under normal circumstances it would have required reasonably careful negotiation. Gerald, steering with one hand while the other hovered over the headlight button on the steering column, found it took all of his powers of concentration simply to keep the big car on the road. Heeding Jaf's sarcastic comment, he rested the Colt Special on the dashboard in front of him. Fraser spoke again out of the gloom.

'Right, Gerry, we're almost there so listen carefully. The best place to ambush a vehicle will be just at the entrance to the grounds because it would have to slow down to a crawl to negotiate the turn-off. Now, if Wilkinson has not shown up yet and these people are still laying in wait for him they will automatically go for the first vehicle which appears. With a bit of luck they won't know we've arrived until we are right on top of them. So, when you swing into that entrance, slam your foot to the floor, switch on your headlights and stop for nothing. OK?'

Gerald nodded. 'OK,' he muttered.

'Right, get ready.' The gateway, like a missing front tooth, loomed suddenly on their right. 'Go, Gerry,' Jaf bellowed. 'And keep your fucking head down.'

Parkinson, acting purely reflexively, slammed his foot to the floor and wrenched the wheel savagely round. Like a greyhound from the trap the big Jaguar leaped forward into a shrieking, rubber-burning turn and, like a missile, headed for the gateway.

Gerald, fighting the wheel, flicked on the headlights. Two men, halfway across the driveway, were halted in midstride by the unexpected white glare and the sudden roar of the car's engine. Like mesmerised rabbits they remained frozen in the headlights, their white faces staring into the glaring eyes of the metal monster hurtling towards them only a few yards away. The speeding Jaguar sideswiped one of the two massive granite pillars flanking the entrance and the shrieking of tortured metal appeared to break the spell. Belatedly they began to move.

The racing vehicle slammed into them like a tank.

Gerald had time to see both men were armed before the nearest of the pair vanished below the wheels. The low slung vehicle lurched sickeningly in the same moment as it struck the second man. For Parkinson everything seemed to slip into slow motion. He felt, rather than heard, the thud of the impact. The man, his gun falling away from nerveless hands, rose up over the bonnet and sailed towards the windscreen. Almost detachedly he observed the wide, staring eyes in the broad Slavic face and saw the mouth open in a gaping, soundless scream. Then the face struck the windscreen splitting open like a rotten tomato the instant before the weight of the flying body forced it through the glass in a shower of tiny, glittering fragments. The man hung half-in, half-out, of the careering vehicle.

Fragments of the flying glass struck Gerald's face and he was immediately aware of the warm rush of blood. But his eyes were undamaged. He could still see over the dangling body as the car continued its crazy rush. Struggling with the madly bucking wheel he was barely aware of the rise and fall of Jaf's arm and the soggy, crunching thud of the gun butt against the dangling head before with a powerful heave the big man forced the body back out of the car. Gerald saw it whip, arms and legs flailing, over the bonnet and vanish.

Then the guns opened up.

He heard and felt the thudding impact of the bullets before one of the front tyres blew and he was fighting again to prevent the car from streaking off the drive and smashing into one of the trees. Another tyre went. The Jaguar spun crazily on its axis and stalled.

Jaf's hand reached across him and cut the lights.

'Out, Gerry,' the big man roared. 'Run for the fucking trees.'

Then suddenly he was out of the car and running madly for the cover of the trees. From somewhere to his left another gun opened up with a stuttering snarl. He heard a hoarse cry from the entrance somewhere, then Jaf's huge hand closed on his arm and the big man hauled him into the safety of the trees. Panting, they flung themselves down behind the bole of a huge chestnut. Fraser's mouth was close to his ear.

'Wilkinson gave us covering fire. Sounded like he might have got one of the bastards too. But as near as I can place him he's on the wrong side of the stream. He's on *this* side and it sounds as if they've got an army over here. If he wants to get out of here alive he's got to get back over the water. There doesn't appear to be any of them over there. See if you can spot the muzzle flashes and let's see what the fuck we've got ourselves into here.'

Wilkinson saw the headlights of the car on the driveway and knew instantly what had happened. An ambush had been laid for him and someone else had been unfortunate to drive into it. Nevertheless with the enemy's eyes focussed on the intruding vehicle the opportunity was ideal for him to get across the bridge unseen. From there he should be able to make the house easily enough and get his hands on some decent weaponry.

Picking up one of the Kalashnikovs he raced for the bridge. He was on home ground now and had taken pains to learn its contours. Pounding across the bridge he heard the car's engine die and saw the lights cut off abruptly. Without stopping to think he sent a short burst into the gateway area. If there was anyone left alive in the car it would at least keep the ambushers' heads down and give the survivors time to take cover.

Sergei Petrovitch, like his comrades momentarily startled by the appearance of the car, did not, however, allow it to distract him more than a moment. He caught the burst of fire from the bridge and guessed immediately who had fired it.

'Lights,' he bellowed frantically. 'Lights!'

Instantly the headlights of the three large cars carefully concealed among the trees blazed into life. The long, rustic bridge across the stream was immediately illuminated as if floodlit. A few feet from the end of the bridge a burly figure dressed in black whirled suddenly and opened fire on the blazing headlights. What was left in the magazine of the captured Kalashnikov tore half Sergei Petrovitch's chest away, and he never heard the drivers of the concealed vehicles open up and send a hail of fire towards the lone figure on the bridge.

From behind the chestnut, Gerald Parkinson quite clearly saw white splinters leap from the woodwork of the bridge. Saw the black figure jolt suddenly and slam back against the handrail and drop the Kalashnikov. Watched a white hand whip across the black body and, incredibly trying to bring a handgun to bear on his attackers, collapse on the plank decking in an attitude almost of prayer. Almost immediately the kneeling figure was lifted to its feet and punched back against the handrail once more, there to slide like a drunken man on to his backside and keel over on his side.

Incensed at the killing for some reason, Gerald was never aware of springing to his feet. But suddenly he was running frantically towards the bridge. Behind him he was remotely aware of Jaf's astonished roar followed by the sharp crack of the M52 as the big man tried to cover his flight. The ripping snarl of automatic weapons ceased suddenly then, as his foot touched the planking of the bridge, someone, possibly clearing a few rounds from his magazine, opened up once more.

Gerald was aware of an enormous hammer-like blow high in his back which hurled him forward across the legs of the sprawled black figure. Incredibly the figure beneath him stirred slightly. Faintly, as he slipped headlong into an abyss, Gerald Parkinson was aware of a gurgling whisper saying 'Shaitan', then there was nothing.

Epilogue

For some reason the shoot-out at Abbey House was never reported in the Press. Seven men including the man known as HAWL died there but the British public were never appraised of that fact. Today the house is owned by a bright young man in the electronics business and neither he, nor his wife and two children, have ever learned what caused the odd damage to the footbridge across the stream.

Two days following the HAWL shoot-out Anne Parkinson received a small package. It contained a beautifully made gold chain, suspended on which was a small plastic and gold cylinder which contained a tightly wrapped ten pound note. Miss Parkinson's renowned report, 'After the Bombing', later won her a much coveted Emmy award.

Gerald Parkinson recovered consciousness in the intensive care unit of a Bath hospital to find Sir Thomas Griff hovering anxiously over his bed. He resigned from Griff's service immediately. His resignation was promptly refused on the strange grounds that the Sphinx had survived for five thousand years. On his release from hospital Parkinson immediately proposed to Miss Moira Fraser and was promptly, and joyfully, accepted. They were married three weeks later.

On the instructions of Sir Thomas Griff, the body of William Wilkinson was quietly buried beside his wife and daughter. It was assumed by the few people who attended the funeral that Wilkinson had finally succeeded in drinking himself to death.

James Alistair Fraser, seeing his daughter happily settled, returned to his calling and little more was heard of him.

Some two weeks following the death of Bill Wilkinson a series of daring robberies took place in large London stores packed with Christmas shoppers. All of these robberies were carried out by one man, said to be very tall.

Three months following the Abbey House affair, a secret terrorist training camp at a place called Wadi Shaitan in South West Libya was bombed with napalm from a helicopter bearing Libyan markings. Sixty-one would-be terrorists died. This information was relayed by telephone to Tim Carter of the *Express.*